One

Thursday, May 5th, 1904

'The man's a spy!' said George. 'I know he's a spy.'

Lydia bit her lip, telling herself not to rise to the bait.

George went on, a note of triumph in his voice: 'He's a spy if ever I saw one! You know it, Lydia, but you can't or won't admit it!'

'That's enough, Father.' She tried to concentrate on her sewing, tried to ignore him, tried to pretend that he was not deliberately upsetting her and tried as usual to make allowances for him. The cotton in her needle ran out, and she finished off and reached for the cotton reel to cut another length of thread.

From the corner of her eye she saw him glance towards her, his eyes searching her face for any sign that he was reaching her with his accusations. She sighed, praying for patience. He was no longer the father she

5

had loved as a child, but that was not his fault.

Four-year-old Adam, sitting between them on the floor with a wooden engine, looked up at her. 'What is a spy, Mama?'

'Nothing,' Lydia answered, her tone sharper than she'd intended. 'A spy is nothing. Don't take any notice of Grandpapa. He's being foolish.'

Foolish and sometimes spiteful, she added silently. Today he was not in a good mood, and at times like today Lydia worried about his influence on her young son.

The old man leaned forward towards the child. 'A spy is a nasty man who does horrid things! A spy betrays the people who trust him. He betrays his country. He—'

Adam looked at her anxiously. 'Is Papa a nasty man?'

'Certainly not! He's a very nice man. Your papa is the best man in the world – and you're the best little boy!' She gave him a reassuring smile. 'Grandpapa is only teasing us.'

'I'm not teasing you, Adam. I'm telling you that—'

Lydia's patience was exhausted. She sprang to her feet, tossed her sewing on to the chair she had just vacated and, reaching for her son, pulled him to his feet. Trying to

6

keep her voice level she said, 'We'll go to the park, shall we, Adam, and you can play on the swings.'

The boy's face lit up at the prospect. 'Will we see the man with the puppy?'

'Maybe.'

Her father said, 'I spy, with my little eye...' and chuckled.

Adam gave him a quick glance and, puzzled by his words, snatched up his teddy bear, ran from the room and up the stairs.

Lydia followed him in a swirl of angry skirts and furious thoughts and almost slammed the door behind her. But that would have given her father great satisfaction. At least she could deny him that.

George laughed when he heard the front door close behind them. 'Deny it as much as you like, my dear daughter, but you know it's the truth. The man you married is not what he seems! Never has been, but you wouldn't be told. Even now you refuse to see the signs.'

Just fifty years old, George Meecham was physically in good health but for the last year his mind had been letting him down. He was becoming confused and was struggling to cling on to what remained of his sanity.

He was sorry he had upset his daughter,

but he reminded himself that he had always been able to spot a wrong'un and he didn't trust his son-in-law one inch and sometimes he found himself voicing his suspicions.

'If only I could keep it to myself,' he groaned. 'It's not her fault, but it's not mine either.' The words came tumbling from his mouth, from his subconscious, and he recalled with a prickle of fear that the same thing had happened to his father in his later years.

Now, uncomfortably reminded of their common failing, George tried to console himself by a litany of things he *could* remember – like his name and address and the fact that he had once been a grocer, like his father before him. Yes. He nodded. His father had been a very successful grocer, who'd died leaving three shops in and around Brockley in south London and a very respectable house in which they now lived.

Closing his eyes, George could remember serving a customer with biscuits from the deep tin in which the assorted biscuits were arranged in layers – one of each type in each layer so that no one could complain that he had given them all the 'boring' ones. He smiled. He could recall the smell of the bacon as he sliced it and the sight of the dried plums laid out in their boxes and the

THE GREAT BETRAYAL

A tale of family, secrets and lies,
from a well-loved author

1904, London. Lydia Daye adores her husband John, but his secret government job means he is often away. She consoles herself with her small son, Adam, and the knowledge that John's salary allows them to live comfortably. Dolly Ellerway lives just two miles away, but in a different world. Pregnant, she is delighted when the father of her child says he'll marry her, even though he can barely afford it. It seems unlikely that the two will ever meet, but one day Lydia sends a fateful letter that will change both women's lives forever...

*Recent Titles by Pamela Oldfield
from Severn House*

The Heron Saga
BETROTHED
THE GILDED LAND
LOWERING SKIES
THE BRIGHT DAWNING

ALL OUR TOMORROWS
EARLY ONE MORNING
RIDING THE STORM

DANGEROUS SECRETS
INTRICATE LIAISONS
TURNING LEAVES

SUMMER LIGHTNING
JACK'S SHADOW
FULL CIRCLE
FATEFUL VOYAGE
THE LONGEST ROAD
THE FAIRFAX LEGACY
TRUTH WILL OUT
THE BIRTHDAY PRESENT
THE BOAT HOUSE
THE PENNINGTONS
THE GREAT BETRAYAL

THE GREAT BETRAYAL

Pamela Oldfield

Severn House Large Print
London & New York

This first large print edition published 2013
in Great Britain and the USA by
SEVERN HOUSE PUBLISHERS LTD of
19 Cedar Road, Sutton, Surrey, England, SM2 5DA.
First world regular print edition published 2012 by
Severn House Publishers Ltd., London and New York.

British Library Cataloguing in Publication Data

Oldfield, Pamela. author.
  The great betrayal. -- Large print edition.
  1. Great Britain--Officials and employees--Family
relationships--Fiction. 2. Pregnant women--Fiction.
3. Life change events--Fiction. 4. London (England)--
Social conditions--20th century--Fiction. 5. Great
Britain--History--Edward VII, 1901-1910--Fiction.
6. Large type books.
I. Title
823.9'14-dc23

ISBN-13: 9780727896506

Severn House Publishers support the Forest Stewardship
Council™ [FSC™], the leading international forest certification
organisation. All our titles that are printed on FSC certified paper
carry the FSC logo.

MIX
Paper from
responsible sources
FSC
www.fsc.org FSC® C013056

Printed and bound in Great Britain by
T J International, Padstow, Cornwall.

new-laid eggs in the straw-filled baskets in which the farmer had delivered them.

'In Parmettor Street.' He opened his eyes. 'Our first shop was in Parmettor Street ... or was that our house? Is *this* Parmettor Street?' To make sure he knew where he was, he crossed to the window and looked down, and sure enough he saw the familiar red pillar box on the opposite pavement and the young plane trees which decorated the street. 'Yes. Good. *This* is Parmettor Street.'

But he had momentarily forgotten the name of the woman he married who gave him his daughter, Lydia, and a son. Now what was the boy's name? Frowning, he tried to concentrate. Sometimes a little effort produced a glimmer, but today it failed to produce anything of any value – until suddenly the name Robert came to him.

He gave a triumphant chuckle. Yes. Robert! That was it. So where was he now? 'Robert, Robert,' he muttered. 'Wherefore art thou, Robert?'

Damned memory! It could summon up a quote from Shakespeare, but could not supply any information about his missing son. He shook his head. Robert seemed to have disappeared somewhere in the half-forgotten past, but how or why was a mystery to him now, and Lydia hated to be questioned about her brother. In fact, she hated to be questioned about anything, he thought resentfully.

'Especially her absent husband!'

In his more lucid moments George could see that it must be irritating for her, but now he sighed, rubbing his head as though that might stimulate the return of some long-lost memories. Yes. Robert, the golden boy. He had somehow slipped away ... but there was a photograph, wasn't there? Or had he dreamed that?

Pushing himself up from the chair he set off in search of it, but instead he wandered into the kitchen with the vague idea of making himself a pot of tea – but once there he forgot about the tea, and a few moments later he found himself in the lavatory where he stood staring out of the small window into the small back garden.

His wife was dead, and he was at the mercy of his daughter. And there was the grandson, Adam, who should have been the light of his life. That's what grandchildren were supposed to be. But there was something wrong somewhere, and he and the boy did not properly relate to each other. The little boy seemed rather afraid of him for some obscure reason. George blamed the man his daughter had married. If the son-in-law was

10

a spy then little Adam was the son of a spy ... He closed his eyes.

'My name is George Douglas Meecham, I am fifty years old and ... and my darling daughter married a spy!' he muttered, his face crinkling with sudden glee. She might deny it a thousand times but *he knew*.

Lydia walked at a brisk pace in an attempt to keep up with Adam who was bowling a wooden hoop along the pavement. Her face was set in unhappy lines as she did her best to forget and forgive her father's latest outburst. She recognized that he was getting old and moving into a twilight world, and for much of the time she tried to overlook his little cruelties. Her mother had loved him, she reminded herself again and again, and for her sake she would try to forgive him.

Adam waited ahead of her, standing on the edge of the pavement, obediently turning his head left and then right, watching the traffic. Lydia took his hand, and when it was safe, they hurried across to the pavement on the far side. Only another hundred yards and they had reached the park and were through the gates. Adam ran off with his hoop, shrieking with excitement, in the direction of the playground.

Lydia followed, keeping an eye out for bad-tempered dogs who might bother her son, or suspicious men who might offer him a lollipop and then snatch him and run off with him to goodness knows where. The fact that John had to be away so much of the time laid a heavy burden of responsibility on her shoulders.

When they reached the playground itself there were perhaps twenty children of various ages enjoying the swings, the slide and the roundabout. Mothers or nannies sat about on the surrounding seats from where they could watch the youngsters.

Lydia sat down on an empty seat, and at once the unwanted questions flooded her mind. Was John a spy? Had he lied to her? Had she been too gullible when they first met, willing to believe everything he told her about himself and his work?

She smiled as Adam returned to pass the hoop into her care.

'The puppy man is here!' he cried, his brown eyes shining. 'From the paper shop. May I go and see the puppy?'

Lydia searched the little crowd and found 'the puppy man' not ten yards away, near the roundabout. 'You may, but don't go any further,' she told him.

When Adam reached him, the man smiled and tousled the boy's hair before turning to look for his mother. When he caught sight of Lydia he raised a hand in greeting. It was Richard Wright from the paper shop.

Never losing sight of her son, her thoughts returned to her husband, whom she still adored. John Daye, tall, dark and handsome, was the only man she had ever loved and she had been willing to accept the fact that, due to his work for the government, their married life would not be easy. He travelled for the government on various assignments which were vital to the safety of the realm. He had explained right from the start that he had signed the Official Secrets Act and could never discuss the work that took him away from home for weeks at a time. He had a passport, and that was proof in her eyes that he was what he said he was – an important member of a government team, working as a departmental courier, carrying documents of a discreet nature up and down the length of Britain and sometimes across the channel.

Naturally, she missed him when he was away, but as he had gently reminded her, he earned a very good salary and they lived better than many. When her mother had died, John had raised no objections to them moving into her old family home to care for her widowed father. At least she had her son, who was a source of great joy.

Lydia frequently reminded herself that with her husband's child beside her, she could never be lonely.

Lost in her thoughts she saw Adam coming towards her, proudly holding the Labrador puppy's lead with Richard Wright close behind him. Smiling, she stood up to greet them, then leaned down to make a fuss of the puppy, which was leaping about hysterically on the end of his lead and making a surprising amount of noise for a dog of his size.

Adam said, 'His name's Snip. Isn't that a nice name? Snip likes me. Mr Wright told me he does.'

Richard Wright grinned down at the boy. 'Oh, he does, yes. He was hoping you'd be here today. He was in the middle of his breakfast, and he stopped and asked me if you would be in the park.'

'Did he?' Thrilled by the news and never doubting it, Adam's eyes shone as he bent down to the puppy. 'Well, here I am, Snip!' He patted the puppy, which licked his hand and made him laugh. He said, 'I can't have a pet because they make Papa sneeze. Not even a mouse in a cage!' He glanced up at Mr Wright. 'Not even a rabbit in a hutch outside.'

Lydia shrugged. 'It's a shame, but it's just

one of those things,' she said, and then she asked after the man's wife, who had had a recent fall and injured her arm.

'It's slightly infected. The doctor reckons it will mend,' he explained, 'but these things take time. How's your husband?'

She kept her voice level. 'I'm afraid John's still away on business.' She sat down again, indicating that he might share the seat with her if he wished. He accepted, and they sat together, watching the antics of the boy and the dog.

Eventually, he said, 'I haven't seen your father in the shop for some time now. Is he worse?'

Her grey eyes darkened. 'I'm afraid so. I try to dissuade him from going outside the house without me in case he gets lost. He could wander away. The doctor has explained that he will never improve so I must expect a steady deterioration in his condition.' She sighed. 'I know my father doesn't mean to be unkind, and I try to make allowances for his behaviour because I know it is part of the disease. We used to be close, but now it's impossible. He has good days and bad days. I do my best, but it is certainly very trying at times and I worry about the effect he has on young Adam ... Still, worse troubles at sea!' She forced a smile.

15

'He's fortunate to have such a caring daughter.' Mr Wright stood up. 'I must get back or my wife will grumble at me! She has extra work to do now that my aunt is staying with us for a few weeks.' He rolled his eyes. 'But she doesn't really mind. Aunt Gladys is very talkative, but they get along well enough and my wife enjoys a bit of female company.'

Adam bade a reluctant farewell to the puppy, and Richard Wright headed back towards the gate. While Adam returned to the roundabout and then the slide, Lydia decided she would write again to her husband, sounding cheerful and positive. She liked to think that when he returned to the office from which he worked, he would find several letters from her and imagined that reading and replying to them would be something he looked forward to.

PSD, Third Floor, Sixteen Mansoor Street, Clerkenwell, London. That was where he was when he was not with her, unless he was away on an assignment. The initials stood for Public Security Department. A modest-sounding address that would arouse no unwelcome attention from the wrong people. That was how John had described it, and it made perfect sense. She liked to imagine him in his office, gravely discussing the current project, serious men huddled round a table, dealing with important matters of state.

Half an hour later, as she and Adam walked home, she was already planning her letter. She could tell John about the walk to the park and Adam and the new puppy at the paper shop, and she would pretend her father had had a better than usual day. No point in depressing him, she told herself. He had an important job to do and worries of his own and reading her letters should be the highlight of his day.

The following morning, less than two miles away, Jenny Ellerway, known by all and sundry as Dolly, hurried from her home at number fifteen, crossed to the house immediately opposite and, as always, banged the knocker four times and held her finger on the bell until the door was opened by Sidney. He was rubbing his eyes, tired from a rough night's sleep after a late supper of pigs' trotters, and was in no mood to exchange niceties.

'He's not here, Doll!' he told her and tried to shut the door, but Dolly Ellerway, anticipating this move, already had her foot over the door sill.

'Course 'e's ere!' She tossed her tangled curls indignantly. 'Where else would he be?'

'He's not here, I tell you. Now hop it, there's a good gal.'

Sidney Wickham was tallish, with dark brown hair and a face that was not remotely handsome, his nose being a little too big and his dark eyes set too close together. When he was born, the story went, his mother thought she had given birth to a goblin.

Dolly laughed. 'What if I don't 'op it?' She stood with her hands on her hips. 'He said he'd be back yesterday and would be over first thing today. Now it's half past seven and I'm going to be late for work! If I get me cards it'll be all his doing. He's in there, isn't he?'

'He's not! Get your foot out of the door!'

'What if I won't?'

He kicked it half-heartedly.

'Then where is he?'

Sidney shrugged. 'I'm his brother, not his bloomin' keeper!'

Before he realized what she was about, she thrust herself past him and shouted up the stairs: 'Oi! Don! Get yourself down 'ere, toot sweet!'

'Toot sweet?'

'French, to you, Sid! Means "get a move on"!' She grinned.

Sidney wavered. The grin made her look sixteen instead of twenty. 'Who are you kid-

18

ding!' He leaned back against the door jamb, yawned, scratched his head and felt suddenly confident that the day was going to be a good one. Not that he'd see much of it. He would idle his way through at least half of it before setting out in search of the bookie's runner, who would take his bet with his usual lack of interest. Then it was round to the Hare and Hounds for a drop of ale.

Dolly cupped her hands to her mouth and yelled, 'Donald John Wickham! It's me, Dolly! Your one true love!'

Sidney put a hand to his eyes, wincing at the noise. 'Must you?' he asked, not expecting an answer. 'He's not back. I told you that. When he does get back I'll tell him you—'

'He calls me that – his one true love! And dearest and sweet'eart!'

'And you fell for it.' He glanced at her swelling belly.

'What if I did?'

'More fool you.'

But she was already hurrying up the bare stairs, her skirt clutched in one hand, and he heard her open and shut the doors along the landing. 'If you're hiding, Don...'

Sidney muttered, 'He's not hiding, you silly crumpet! He's not back yet.' Women! What was it about his brother that he always

19

got the best-looking women – without even trying?

Dolly clattered down the stairs, her face flushed, but whether with anger or disappointment he could not say. 'Tell him I'll be by on my way home – and God 'elp 'im if he's not back!' She threw him a mocking kiss and was away.

For someone in her state – six months gone – she had a sight too much energy, he reflected. Then he grinned. His brother certainly could pick 'em!

The Pig and Whistle was the favourite haunt of many of the labourers around St Katharine's Dock, and that was where Donald Wickham expected to find Willis Burke, known as 'the reverend' to his mates. Willis Burke had originally come from a nice God-fearing family, who'd doted on their only son, a gentle child with soft brown hair, large grey eyes, a sweet nature and a willingness to attend Sunday school. Unfortunately, Willis had cut himself adrift when they'd decided he would make a wonderful 'man of the cloth'. To please them, he had at first agreed to attend St Joseph's College, to study Religious History and Divinity with the intention of entering the church. He had soon realized, however, that he was not the man they thought he was and had made a big mistake.

Firstly, he had struggled with the syllabus, and secondly, he had found himself totally uninterested. He had decided that pleasing his family was not the way he needed to go so, reluctantly, he had broken his parents' hearts, left home and had been immediately drawn into the shifting sands that made up a large part of London's casual workforce.

Seven years after abandoning his original plan and several more plans, he found himself existing on casual employment in and around the docks, but the peanuts he earned currently as a nightwatchman in a warehouse were swollen by what he liked to see as his 'little sideline'.

When Don caught up with him in the Pig and Whistle he was sipping a pint of ale and looking forward to his bed.

As Don sat down beside him, Burke said, 'Whatever it is, the answer's no!' but he reached for the second pint that Don carried, which he guessed was for him and was obviously meant as a sweetener. What did the man want now, he wondered.

Don said, 'I think you're getting uglier, Reverend, or is it the light?'

'I work at it! What's your excuse?'

Around them the noise blossomed suddenly as a man came into the bar with a dog which was immediately challenged by the resident mongrel. Heads turned to watch the fight, and as the dogs' scrabbling paws flicked up dirty sawdust, the customers took sides and began to cheer on their favourites. The barman ignored the rumpus, which ended abruptly when the intruder slipped his collar and both dogs tumbled into the street and nearly upturned a costermonger's barrow loaded with muddy potatoes.

Don lowered his voice. 'As I was saying, Reverend, I've got a nice little proposition for you.' He rubbed finger and thumb together. 'Bit of extra cash. Take it or leave it.'

'The answer's no, and don't keep calling me "reverend". I keep telling everyone – I've given all that up. You know I have.'

'I know you think you have, and we admire you for it. You did the right thing. Look at you now – a wonderful job, generous pay and a charming little attic room where you can sleep all day!' He drank deeply.

The sarcasm was not lost on Burke. Bright enough to know that he was being mocked, he scowled. 'For God's sake! I don't do that stuff any more. I don't know why people keep asking me. Look what it got me before. Three months in Pentonville for fraud. A hellhole if ever there was one!' His voice was rich with indignation, but a small part of him was sorely tempted. If truth were told, Willis loved dressing up as a 'reverend'. He felt it had once been a glorious future, which had been snatched away from him in a moment of his own youthful weakness. If only his parents had insisted. If only his tutors had begged him not to give up the Lord's work...

Tutting, Don shook his head. 'Prison. That was disgraceful, that was! Shocking! A true miscarriage of justice ... Come on, Reverend. Drink up. You've time for one more.'

'Never turn down a drink' was one of Burke's mottoes, so he obligingly emptied his tankard and Don caught the barmaid's eye as she waltzed past.

'Same again, Prue, my lovely!'

'It's Sue!' But she fluttered her lashes at him.

'Sue or Prue – you're just as pretty!' He turned his attention back to Burke and the matter in hand. 'There's this young lady...' he began.

'God Almighty!' Burke groaned. 'What did I just say? You got cloth ears or what?'

'You said you've given up doing all that stuff ... but I'm a mate, and there's a sweet young lady in trouble – if you know what I mean – and a tenner in it for you. Ten bob! Ten shillings. She's in the family way, and I just want to do the right thing by her. You know how it is. You're a man of the world, Reverend, and you're not stupid enough to turn your back on ten shillings.'

Burke was still shaking his head when the next round appeared, but he snatched at his pint before Don could change his mind. He was still telling himself that this time he meant 'no'. The time in prison had taught him a severe lesson. He was determined not to repeat past mistakes, and that meant resisting the wiles of men like Don Wickham ... but he owed four weeks' rent, and it would make sense financially to say yes.

Don leaned forward and raised his ale in a sign of celebration. 'Cheers and down the hatch!' he said. 'You'll be making a young lady very happy.'

Burke made up his mind. He'd do it, but he'd make it worth his while. 'I haven't said I'll do it, and I won't do it!' he said firmly. 'Get it into your head, will you? I'm not doing that fake religious stuff any more. I don't want to get into trouble again. The screws said, "You'll be back!" and I said "Never, on my mother's grave!" and they...'

'But you *will* do it.' Don grinned at him and leaned across confidingly. 'Tell you what, Reverend, because it's you, and you certainly aren't the best-paid nightwatch-

24

man in London, I'll double it. How's that?'

'Double it?' Burke nearly choked on his ale.

'Twenty shillings!'

'I dunno.'

'Come on, Reverend. You could pay off the rent you owe and ... and get your stuff out of hock.'

'Wait a minute!' He looked at Don suspiciously. 'How d'you know about all that?'

'Because everyone's in the same boat! Everyone's in hock, and everyone owes the landlord.'

'I bet you don't.'

'You'd be surprised. But *if* I'm not in debt it's because I use this!' He tapped his head. 'So what d'you say, eh? You'd be a fool to say "no", and you aren't a fool, are you?'

Knowing Wickham, Burke now suspected that the man had halved his offer first time round ... but so what? He would do it – this one last time and never again. 'Throw in a pork pie and it's a deal!' he offered. 'But you'll have to keep it under your hat! I'm not going back inside for a measly twenty shillings.'

'Not a word of it will ever pass my lips!' Don thrust out his hand. 'Shake on it, Reverend. It's a deal.'

★ ★ ★

That same afternoon, on her way home from shopping, Lydia decided to try her father with the photographs. Seeing the members of the family in black and white might jog his memory and make him feel more confident. She was hoping that being less vague and more 'in control' might restore some of the good humour she recalled from times past. Dour he certainly was and often had been, but her mother had explained that some people did not know how to be happy. At least Lydia knew that he had once loved her.

She found him in the potting shed, scraping soil from a stack of flower pots, and coaxed him back into the house with the promise of a pot of tea and biscuits.

When she judged the time to be right, she said, 'Shall we look at the photographs, Adam? You like that, don't you?'

Delighted, he abandoned his colouring book and hurried importantly to the sideboard to collect the album.

Lydia said, 'If we can't remember all the names, Grandpapa will have to help us.'

The boy settled beside her on the sofa, and Lydia was pleased to see her father edge his chair a little closer to them.

'Here we go!' said Lydia, opening the album to reveal the first photograph. 'Now who are these people, Adam?'

He pointed with a stubby finger. 'That's Grandpapa, and that's Grandmama but now she's gone to heaven.'

Lydia said, 'Let's ask Grandpapa if you are right,' and looked at him enquiringly.

With feigned reluctance he leaned closer and nodded. 'That's me and...' He closed his eyes. 'I ought to know her name,' he muttered. It's ... It's ... Estelle?'

Adam looked at his mother for approval.

'Nearly right,' she told them. 'Grandmama's name was Elspeth.'

'Elspeth?' George repeated. 'But that's what I said. Elspeth. Yes. Of course it was. Taken two months after our marriage.'

'Well done!' said Lydia, and Adam, taking his cue, clapped his hands.

She turned the page to a formal portrait of herself and her brother, taken on Robert's eleventh birthday. 'And these two children are...?'

George leaned closer, frowning. 'So that's where he got to,' he said, speaking to himself. 'Robert! Yes, of course. That's Robert. He's in the album.' He glanced up at his daughter. 'Where did he get to? I never see him these days.'

Adam said eagerly, 'He was my uncle, but he was only little in the picture, and then he was knocked down by a big, big horse and...'

27

George gave a strangled cry and struggled to his feet. 'That's enough, young Adam,' he said harshly. 'You never knew him like I did! He was a wonderful boy. Wonderful, d'you hear me? Something about a horse...? Yes, that was it. Knocked down in his prime! Such a waste.' His face crumpled.

Dismayed, Lydia closed the album with a snap and whispered to Adam to replace it in the sideboard. She turned to her father and said gently, 'Robert had a happy life, Father. We shouldn't mourn him. He wouldn't wish it. He—'

George steadied himself with one hand on the mantelpiece and glared at his daughter. 'Don't try to tell me he's gone. I know better. He's ... he's around. You'll see ... Robert. Yes, that's it.'

Sensing the change of atmosphere, Adam closed the sideboard door and looked towards his mother for reassurance.

She said, 'Father, you have a wonderful grandson! If you would only take the time to get to know him, Adam would...'

He waved the suggestion away with a sweep of his free hand. 'His father's a spy!' he said. 'Don't try to fool me.'

She bit back a reproach, telling herself that he scarcely knew what he was saying and was not to blame for his cruel outburst. As he

wandered out into the passage, still mum-
bling angrily to himself, Lydia, with tears in
her eyes, swept Adam into her arms and
hugged him.

Two

The next morning the postman brought a letter from Lydia's husband, and she rushed upstairs to read it in private. Later she would read carefully selected passages to her son and father. Seating herself by the window, she kissed the envelope, tore it open and drew out the enclosed letter.

'Only two sheets!' she murmured, disappointed, but she then reminded herself that two pages were better than none at all and that John was a very busy man.

My dearest Liddy. At last I can snatch a few moments to write to you. I have been desperately busy, but I console myself that you are a wonderfully understanding wife and I am a lucky man.

'A wonderfully understanding wife!' she echoed, drawing a little comfort from the compliment.

Thank you so much for your letters, which are always a source of joy to me when I find time to return to the office before dashing off again.

Please thank Adam for the picture he sent of a train engine. Maybe he will grow up to be a train driver. Stranger things have happened.

Lydia smiled. Her son's attempt had consisted of a very small yellow engine surrounded by billowing blue smoke.

Now that I am back in London I can finish the business and hurry home. This should reach you on Friday and I expect to be arriving on your doorstep soon after – by Monday, I hope. What a lot of 'catching up' we shall have to do, my darling. You cannot know how much I miss you when we are apart. And little Adam will be growing fast. Give him a kiss from me and tell him I shall bring him a present if he has been a good boy...

Lydia let out a deep sigh of contentment. He was coming home and he loved her and was anxious to see his son. What more could she ask of him, she wondered happily.

I do hope your father is no worse. We both know he is not to blame but you must find him difficult, dearest, and no doubt he will grow worse, but if we are ever rich you shall have a nurse to help you care for him.

No more now, my dearest Lydia. Fondest love from your loving husband John.

Lydia folded the letter and pressed it to her heart. Not long to wait, she told herself, and their little family would be complete again.

31

A few moments later she went downstairs, where Adam was crawling along the floor, pushing a painted wooden boat, and her father was reading *The Times*. The latter glanced up as she came in, his face alight with interest, and she was reminded how he used to look when he was younger, before the deterioration had set in.

'Would you credit it?' he demanded. 'Another armed robbery – this time at Glazers in Oxford Street. Jewellery valued at over a thousand pounds!' He shook his head. '*Over a thousand pounds*! The audacity of it. The sheer effrontery of the thieves. They do say the police have a lead, but then they always say that.'

Lydia raised her eyebrows. 'Do they think it's the same gang?'

He consulted the article. 'Yes. Same *modus operandi*. I'd like to get my hands on the blighters. There were three men: one to drive the getaway car, one to hold up the staff at gunpoint and one to grab the stuff. They didn't shoot anyone this time, but they used a gun to knock one of the customers to the ground and he's in a poor way in hospital with a fractured skull.'

Adam looked up. 'What is a hospital?'

His grandpapa smiled. 'A place where you go if you're ill.'

The boy turned to Lydia.

She said, 'You go to stay there in a cosy little bed and the doctors and nurses make you better again.'

'If you're lucky!' George growled.

Lydia gave her father a warning look, then remembered her letter from John. As soon as she began to read an edited version for her son's sake, her father stood up and threw down his newspaper. 'I can't listen to this nonsense,' he told her. 'Can't believe a word he says! Never could. I warned you.'

'Oh, for heaven's sake!' she snapped, her joy evaporating. 'Please don't start that again, Father.' Her voice rose slightly. 'Poor John has done nothing to deserve your constant criticism.'

'How could he? He's never here! Last Christmas he disappeared in the middle of the Christmas dinner!'

'He was called away on urgent business.'

'So he said – and you chose to believe him! I'll be in the garden if you want me.' Scowling, he pushed himself to his feet.

Adam looked at him. 'But Grandpapa, it's raining!'

'I like the rain.'

Lydia gritted her teeth. 'If you must go in the garden, please take an umbrella, Father.'

'I'll do nothing of the sort. I'll get wet – but

that's my business. My choice! You seem to forget I'm not a child. I'm your father!'

Lydia bit back another sharp reply, but then forced back the words and smiled at her son. 'Come and sit with me, Adam, and I'll read you what Papa says about that picture you drew for him. The engine. Do you remember?'

He beamed as he scrambled on to the sofa beside her. 'The one with all the smoke? Did Papa like it?'

'He liked it very much, Adam.'

'I can draw him another picture. I can draw a house and a tree, and I can put Snip in the picture.'

'I'm sure he would like that, Adam. Your papa is coming home soon, Adam, and you can tell him all about the puppy.'

As the door closed behind her father, Lydia closed her eyes briefly, torn between relief and guilt. She knew he could not help his irritable state of mind – his growing confusion must be terribly trying for him – but his hostility hurt her. If John were ever to become truly rich, which she doubted he would, a kindly nurse to help with her father would be a real blessing.

That same afternoon Dolly sat opposite her beloved in Bert's Caff, listening with disbelief as Don outlined his plan. She sipped her tea without tasting it as her new life unfolded, word by word. In her wildest dreams she had never expected him to actually marry her, but she had hoped they would live together with their baby. Now he was promising to make her his legal wife, and the idea was almost too exciting to bear.

'You mean ... get wed in a church and everything?' She stared at him. 'This isn't a joke, is it? You wouldn't be so cruel ... would you?' Her heart was racing as she tried to imagine herself standing outside the church with their friends around her. Mrs Jenny Wickham! No, what was she thinking? She would be Mrs *Donald* Wickham.

'No, Dolly, this isn't a joke,' he said gently. 'But there won't be a church because that would cost too much money and I'm trying to save up so that later on we can find a little flat and be on our own away from Mansoor Street – maybe an airy attic with a nice view across the rooftops.'

Dolly felt quite faint at the thought of it. She had expected to move in with the two brothers and would have settled for that. A place of their own! She wanted to throw her arms around him and hug the living daylights out of him but restrained herself. There was more to know, and she wanted to hear it all. She looked trustingly into his eyes as he continued.

'I have a very good friend who has promised to marry us – a quiet, private affair with just Sidney as best man ... His name is Reverend Willis Burke, and he has conducted several other weddings. He is not going to charge us the full rate because partly the ceremony will be his present to us. Isn't that splendid of him?'

'His wedding present to us? Oh, that is so kind!' Dolly liked him already. 'Will he – you know ... Will he wear all the right clothes? The long dress and stuff? I mean, will he look like a reverend?'

'Certainly. He *is* a reverend. Everything will be just as you imagine except for the church and all that silly hymn singing. There's a small room over the Rose and Garter on Clarence Street which he uses for these private affairs.'

She had the feeling that he was watching her closely and did not want him to think she was in any way disappointed but she knew the Rose and Garter, and Clarence Street was hardly where she would have chosen to hold their wedding. But ... beggars can't be choosers, she told herself.

Don took hold of her hand. 'Then afterwards we can pop down for a drink and—'

'Can my ma come? And my sister and...'

He shook his head. 'I'm afraid not. The licensing laws only allow weddings on the premises if they are entirely private and discreet. No crowds. No rice or rose petals. They're just trimmings, anyway. A private wedding is a very staid affair. Simple and elegant.'

'But my ma...' Her voice wavered.

'No, Dolly!' His tone had changed. 'I've just explained that a private wedding has to be exactly that. *Private.*' He shrugged, and his expression hardened. 'Look, Dolly, if you would rather skip the wedding it's fine by me. I wanted to please you, that's all. I don't give two damns!'

Dolly gasped. She stared at him, stricken. 'No! No, everything's fine, Don. Fine and dandy.' She forced a smile, terrified that the dream wedding was about to be snatched away. 'Truly it is, Don.' She gazed at him beseechingly. 'We can tell everyone afterwards. Explain that it was private and everything.'

'Good girl. I knew you'd be sensible. We'll be man and wife, and that's all that matters. The baby will have a mother and father. It's arranged for two o'clock on Saturday.' He smiled. 'Promise me you'll be there!'

'Oh dearest Don, most certainly I'll be there – in my best bib and tucker!' She was recovering from her fright. But whatever was she going to wear? she wondered, immediately anxious. Maybe she would confide in her sister and borrow the white silk rose from her straw hat. She could pin that on her Sunday best dress ... But would her sister be able to keep the secret? She was something of a blabbermouth...

'You must tell no one, Dolly,' he was urging. 'The reverend was most particular about that. If word gets out, he'll be pestered from noon 'til dusk by other folk wanting the same – and he'll blame us!'

Suddenly, his eyes darkened again. 'There is one more thing, Dolly, that you must accept. The day after the wedding I am away again on business all day so...'

'On a Sunday?' A wave of regret swept through her at the prospect. 'But if you tell them you've just got married...'

He stood up. 'No, Dolly. There is no way round it. Being a salesman means being available. If a customer in Leeds wants to see our sample range, I'm going to get it to him on time.'

'Can't they send someone else – just this once?'

'They could, but I'm the best they have so it has to be me. Lester's are a very big firm, and we can't afford to disappoint them ...

but if I get the order I'll do what I always do.'

She brightened. 'You'll bring me a present!'

'Cross my heart and hope to die!' He grinned. 'Give me a kiss, you funny girl!'

'I'm not a girl,' she protested, kissing him. 'I'm a mother-to-be!'

'And a bride-to-be!' He held her close and kissed her again. 'Now remember, two o'clock tomorrow, outside the Rose and Garter, and in the twinkling of an eye you'll be Mrs Wickham!'

Meanwhile, alone in his dreary room, Willis Burke was rummaging in his flimsy wardrobe for what he laughingly called his 'vestments' – a long shapeless dress which he had found in a second-hand clothes shop and which had once been white, and a long table runner which he had cleverly redesigned so that it fitted round his neck and shoulders and hung down over the front of his body. The latter, he felt, gave the outfit a certain *gravitas* because it had several tassels remaining along each end. Now he retrieved both items and regarded them dubiously.

They need ironing, he told himself, but he did not own an iron – and even if he did, he could never afford a fire with which to heat it. He could ask his landlady, Mrs Duggett, to iron them, but she might wonder what he was doing with such strange items and she would certainly make a small charge for the work.

It irked him that he had nothing resembling the headgear that vicars sometimes wore – or was that bishops? He ought to know such things, he thought guiltily.

Although Willis knew that impersonating a vicar was risky, he rather enjoyed the thrill of dressing up, and he usually managed to think himself into the role once he was dressed and the bride had arrived. This would be his fifth wedding, and he had only been caught out once. All things considered, he managed to convince himself that it was worth the risk because he was always well paid for the service and the money was very necessary since the nightwatchman's job paid scanty wages.

'Now where the hell is that bible?' he muttered. He felt that once dressed in 'the outfit', holding a bible made the whole charade more believable, and he was proud of the way he could recite an approximation of the service. Now, however, he sighed. Did the women believe in the makeshift service or was the ring on the finger what really mattered? Did they care, one way or the other? Willis Burke had no idea.

He searched the flimsy desk, which did double duty as a table, and peered under the bed, but eventually found the bible under the once handsome sofa, propping up a missing castor. Tutting, he carefully dusted it off. On impulse, he pulled the dress over his head and smoothed it down, trying unsuccessfully to get rid of the creases. Then he draped the table runner over his shoulders. Thus arrayed, he picked up the bible, opened it and smiled at an imaginary couple in what he hoped was a fatherly way.

Willis cleared his throat. 'Dearly beloveds...' he began, then paused to adjust his voice to a more sanctimonious tone. 'We are gathered here to unite these two people in marriage and Holy Matrimony in the face of God who loves all sinners...' He faltered. What else did he have to say? Frowning, he turned the pages of the bible, but came upon nothing that was suitable for the occasion.

'Drat!' Once upon a time the necessary words had just flowed from his lips, but during his incarceration in an unpleasant prison cell his ability to invent had suffered somewhat. He tried again. 'Beloved brethren, here in the sight of the Lord, we ask for your forgiveness...' Forgiveness? For what exactly? He rolled his eyes. For getting married? Or for pretending to do so? And if He was keen to forgive sinners why had He not helped Willis avoid incarceration? Surely He could have weighed in and used his power to rescue his faithful servant!

Giving up, he tossed the book aside and began to parade slowly up and down, wishing he could see himself, but the only mirror was a small one which hung above the chipped sink in the corner. Suddenly inspired, he tried again.

'In the love of the Holy Ghost, the Holy Father and God...' A niggling doubt still lingered, but it was slowly coming back to him. Just a matter of time, he reassured himself. Ah yes! Willis brightened. There would be the ring to deal with. Now how did that bit go? 'Take this woman ... No ... With this ring I declare you man and wife!' But was that it *exactly*? With a sigh he determined to work at it before the bride and groom arrived for the service. He wanted his performance to be faultless.

That afternoon Lydia planned to take Adam along to the paper shop which among other things sold birthday cards, knitting patterns and wools, children's books and a few sweets. These last were to be found in a row of large bottles arranged on the shelves behind the counter. She herself wanted a birthday card for a neighbour – an elderly widowed lady who lived next door but one.

Adam clutched a penny which Lydia had given him to spend on sweets of his choice, and he walked beside his mother feeling very important and trying to imagine which sweets he would spend the penny on.

At the last minute George had decided he needed the exercise and said he would join them on their walk, so the three of them set off together. Lydia did not know whether to be glad or sorry that her father was going with them. He might behave perfectly, or he might do or say something extravagant and entirely unsuitable, or he might wander away altogether while she was otherwise engaged. On the other hand, if he remained at home on his own there was no knowing what mishaps might occur.

When they arrived the shop was very full because the schoolchildren were on their way home and had made the paper shop a last port of call. George surveyed the available newspapers with a critical eye, but turned his attention to the magazines, finally choosing *The Gardener* and paying for it. He then tried to help Adam choose which sweets he would spend his penny on.

'There's a jar of humbugs,' he suggested, pointing to it. 'And next to that is a jar of lemon sherberts – the ones that fizz in your mouth. Do you like those?'

Adam shook his head. 'I sometimes like the sugar mice...' he said, frowning with concentration, 'and I sometimes like the liquorice strips.' From his position on the floor he could hardly see the selection for the throng of schoolchildren who laughed and argued at the tops of their voices.

George suddenly hoisted Adam and rested him on his left hip. 'Now you can see the sweets, Adam.' He chuckled. 'What will it be, eh? You like lollipops, don't you?'

'And pear drops!' the boy said, troubled by so much choice and the responsibility of making a decision. Within minutes, however, a transaction was made, and Adam was returned to the floor where he found Snip the puppy and renewed their acquaintance.

When at last Lydia reached the counter the shop had almost emptied and she and Richard Wright were able to chat.

To her surprise, Mr Wright had a request to make. 'I don't suppose you would consider taking another lodger, Mrs Daye?' he asked. 'A very nice young man came in yesterday enquiring if I knew of anyone who might rent him a room for a few months. He's just moved into the area for his job. A promotion, he told me.'

'Oh no, I don't think so,' Lydia began.

'I just thought because you have quite a big house, and he would only want one room. I'm sure he'd be no trouble, and I know you did have a lodger once...'

'But that was a lady lodger,' Lydia explained. 'She was a friend of my mother's – a spinster – but she was only with us for a year or so.' She was suddenly aware of her father taking an interest in the exchange and lowered her voice. 'I really don't think so. I mean, I would have to consult my husband before I could agree, and I'm sure he would say no...'

George, moving closer, smiled at Mr Wright. 'Nice chap, you say? Well now, I wonder. I wouldn't say no to a little male company.'

Lydia's heart sank. Her father was going to interfere. It was exactly what she had dreaded.

Mr Wright rushed on, now addressing his remarks to her father, who seemed to be more sympathetic to the idea. 'The thing is, the way he explained it, he intended to stay with his cousin who lives somewhere near here with a wife and child but she has suddenly gone down with some sort of kidney disease and cannot now cope with a lodger, not even a family member.'

'I'm sure John won't approve,' Lydia said as firmly as she could in the circumstances. It was her father's house, she reminded herself, so he was entitled to be consulted. 'He might think it improper – him being away so much.'

Mr Wright was looking at her father. 'He buys himself something light at midday – a pie or some such – but would appreciate a cooked meal in the evening ... if you are preparing something for the family, that is. His name's Leonard Phipps.'

'Leonard Phipps.' George looked at Lydia, who was shaking her head. 'I like the sound of Leonard Phipps. What d'you think, Lydia? Should we throw him the proverbial lifeline?'

'I really don't think so, Father. At least, I must talk to John about it, and I'm sure he won't like the idea.'

'Why ever not?' Her father gave her a challenging look. 'Your husband is away so much that he would hardly notice if we had another man around the place! Mr Phipps could have the upstairs room that Miss Baisley used to have—'

'Miss Baisley?'

'Wasn't that her name? The old dear.'

'Her name was Farley. Edith Farley.'

'Well, what's in a name, eh?' he said with a laugh. 'As I was saying, he could have her

46

room and just pop down to dine with us ...
or better still, you could cover the meal with
a cloth and he could carry it up on a tray.'

Lydia felt helpless against the two of them.
'We'd have to meet him first,' she said weak-
ly. 'We might not get along. And I would
definitely have to ask John before I agreed.
And as I'd be the one who'd have to look
after him, I must have *some* say in the matter.'

But Mr Wright was beaming. 'You'd have
to meet, naturally, and agree a price. No
doubt a few extra shillings a week would
come in handy for you. Suppose I send him
round to you next time he calls in? I know
he's very keen to settle somewhere he can
call his own – be it ever so humble! That's
how he put it.' He smiled. To Lydia he said,
'I feel sure you'll approve of him, Mrs Daye,
but if you don't, or if your husband is against
the idea, I'm sure Leonard Phipps will
understand. I'll tell him it's just a possibility.'

George said heartily, 'Well, that's settled,
give or take a few details.' With a cheery nod
to Mr Wright he walked out of the shop,
taking Adam with him.

Lydia was forced to say, 'Goodbye,' and
hurry after them.

Her father was talking to Adam. 'A very
nice man is coming to stay with us. Won't

that be fun?'

Adam, his mouth full of raspberry lollipop, nodded dutifully, but Lydia's spirits sank to a new low. She should have known it would be a mistake to allow her father to accompany them.

Halfway home she brought up the subject again, trying to strike a warning note about the unsuitability of taking a young male lodger into the household. 'We don't know anything about him.'

Her father remained unrepentant. 'How can your husband possibly object when I am here to act as chaperone?' he demanded, laughing heartily at the very idea of anything untoward happening.

'But what about the neighbours? They might talk.'

'Why should they? We don't talk about them.'

'But they're not doing anything to talk about, Father!'

'How do we know that? Look at Mrs Roffey, next door but one. She looks like a sly piece.'

'A sly piece! For heaven's sake, Father! That's a terrible thing to say! Poor Mrs Roffey. She's a grandmother, for goodness' sake. She was once a nursery maid. She's—'

'Mr Stamp then. How do we know what he

gets up to in that motor of his? Driving off every morning to do goodness knows what! Coming home at night as though butter wouldn't melt in his mouth!'

'Mr Stamp is a perfectly respectable railway clerk! I'm quite sure he's not doing anything at all unlawful. He has a wife and two children. He's...'

'Where does he get the money to buy a motor car? He might be a gambling man. He might be a spy.'

'He is not a spy, Father. You have spies on the brain! None of our neighbours are doing anything wrong and—'

'And neither are we!' He gave her a triumphant smile, took off his spectacles and began to polish them with his handkerchief. 'We will simply be offering a nice young man a roof over his head for a few months. A very charitable, very Christian gesture, if you like.'

Lydia regarded her father with dismay. 'You must not go round maligning the neighbours,' she said. 'Promise me you won't repeat any of this nonsense. Someone might sue you for slander – or is it libel? I'm not sure.'

'You're being very silly, Liddy. Anyone who tries to sue me for anything will wonder what has hit them! It's not something I would take lying down, Liddy. I know my rights, and none of my petty neighbours are going to drag me down. Let them take me to court. I relish a good fight!' His eyes shone, and Lydia realized with dismay that he was becoming quite aggressive. She now regretted her careless remarks.

Adam took the lollipop out of his mouth and asked, 'Is Grandpapa going to fight someone?'

'No, dear,' said Lydia. 'Of course not.'

'I might,' said George. He held up two clenched fists and parried an invisible opponent. 'What is it they say? "If push comes to shove!"'

Almost against her will, and confused by her father's arguments, Lydia began to wonder if perhaps she might be worrying too much about the lodger. Was she erring too far on the side of caution? But what on earth would John say?

As if reading her thoughts, George said, 'Your husband ought to be grateful to have another man in the house in case of any trouble. He's always away, off spying somewhere, leaving a helpless wife and child with only an elderly gentleman to protect them! What good would I be if we were burgled?'

None at all, she thought, but said, 'I'm sure you'd do your best, Father.'

'But it wouldn't be good enough, would it, Lydia? And if I rushed to your rescue I might have a heart attack and you'd never forgive yourself!'

His indignation was giving way to something milder, and he gave her such a humorous look that at last she gave in and laughed. 'Very well. If you want this Mr Phipps as a lodger, Father, and if he seems pleasant enough, you'll have to talk to John. He hopes to be home soon.'

'I'll do that then.' He gave her a kindly smile and patted her shoulder.

Lydia hid her surprise and a lump came into her throat and with it the familiar hope. This was the Father she remembered from happier times.

Adam looked up and asked, 'What is a harty tack?'

George smiled. 'He doesn't miss much, does he, this brother of yours?' Leaning down, he gave the boy a friendly tap on the head with his copy of *The Gardener*. 'Nothing for you to worry about, Robert. You just think about that big bridge we're building. We'll have another look at it when we get home.'

'We've still got some bricks left, Grandpapa,' the boy said eagerly. 'We could make the bridge stronger.'

'Good idea, son. We don't want it to fall down, do we?'

And Lydia's hope for an unlikely miracle recovery was once again dashed.

Saturday arrived at last, and Dolly made her way to the place where she and Don were to be wed. The room over the bar at the Rose and Garter was depressingly drab, and she eyed it with dismay as she waited for her groom to arrive. It smelled of stale pipe tobacco and the pomade that some men liked to use to control unruly hair. There were chairs stacked along the wall, a very stained carpet and a long table covered with old green brocade curtains on which someone had placed two half-burned candles – one at either end. In the middle there was a small pot containing a bunch of violets which had obviously been bought from the flower girl who sat day in, day out, outside the Rose and Garter. But at least the man of God impressed her, standing before the altar with his hands clasped and his eyes closed in a prayerful way as though he was thinking religious thoughts. He was younger than she had expected with nice brown hair.

Willis Burke, regal in his impromptu robes, opened his eyes and smiled at her eagerly. 'What do you think, Miss Ellerway?' he asked proudly, indicating the room setting with a modest wave of his hand. 'I think the candles are a nice touch. The landlady lent them to me.' He waved a box of matches. 'We can light them when we start the service.' Dolly nodded. 'And I've brought the bible.' He laughed nervously. 'Mustn't forget that, must we!'

'No.' She tried to ignore the faded wallpaper, which had once been red and gold stripes, and the windows, which needed cleaning.

'Nice violets,' she said and glanced up at the large wall clock that looked as if it might have originated on the platform of a railway station.

The reverend beamed. 'I bought the violets for you. You can take them with you as a memento of your wedding!'

'You're very kind.' She was genuinely touched by the gesture. 'I'll treasure them. Might press them in a book. The colours always fade, but the flowers are still flowers, aren't they?'

He nodded. 'I must say you look very ... bride-like.'

'It's my Sunday best,' she confided, giving a brief twirl to show off the cream jacket and skirt which had been handed down from her sister two years earlier. She had borrowed a friend's white straw hat and had added a scrunched arrangement of cream lace cut from the hem of an old petticoat. At last she glanced at the clock, which confirmed her worst fears. 'He's five minutes late!'

'Five minutes? Oh, that's nothing to worry about, Miss Ellerway. Grooms are often late.' He stifled a yawn. Having been up all night, he was tired, but the excitement of the moment was carrying him along.

After an awkward silence, Willis said, 'Not long now and you won't be Miss Ellerway any more. You'll be Mrs Wickham.'

'I wanted my ma to be here!' she told him, a hint of reproach in her voice. 'And my sister Mavis. Don said it wasn't allowed at a private wedding. They are both going to be disappointed when they know – and very cross with me!'

'Did he? Ah!' Taken aback he said, 'Well ... The thing is...'

'Was he ... bending the truth, Reverend?'

'No, no!' He began to fumble with the matches, lighting the candles, avoiding her eyes. 'It's all to do with ... *with the licence.* Yes, indeed. A private wedding has a different licence, and it means ... Well, it limits everything. Length of service, no bell ringing, no choir. That sort of thing.'

'And no family?'

54

'I believe your husband-to-be is bringing his brother, but then he's the best man. He brings the ring. Very important.' He risked a glance in her direction, hoping he had managed a change of topic.

Before Dolly could answer, there were footsteps on the stairs and along the landing, and the door opened to admit her groom. He looked reasonably well turned out, she thought gratefully, with a clean white shirt, a waistcoat under the jacket, and dark trousers. The shoes lacked polish, but she was willing to overlook that because he was wearing a new hat set at a jaunty angle. He looked like a young 'man about town', she thought proudly.

Smiling shyly, suddenly overcome by the occasion, she said, 'You look really, really nice.'

'So do you, Doll.'

Willis asked, 'Where's the best man?'

'He's in bed with a sick stomach. We can manage without him, *can't we*?' He raised his eyebrows slightly.

Dolly started to protest, but Willis said, 'Certainly. All you need is a man of God.'

Don looked at the reverend. 'Then it's time to get going. Where's the bible?' He winked at Dolly. 'Got to do things properly, haven't we!'

The bible was produced, the young couple were drawn closer together and Willis cleared his throat as he flicked idly through the bible, pretending to find the appropriate page.

Adopting his sanctimonious voice, he began. 'Dearly beloveds, this is a solemn occasion as we join together Miss Ellerway and Mr Wickham in ... in sickness and in health.' Relieved that he had made a good beginning, Willis paused and took a deep breath.

Dolly whispered, 'Can we hold hands?'

He nodded, and Dolly slipped her hand into Don's and squeezed it. It gave her confidence to feel his strong grasp, and she smiled up at him and wondered if the baby might be aware of what was happening.

'We ask the Holy Father, Holy Ghost and Holy Spirit to love and comfort you both...' Willis closed his eyes, held the bible with one hand and crossed himself. Dolly did the same and nudged Don into compliance. 'Do you, Dolly, and you, Donald, take each other in lawful matrimony ... for better for worse and richer and poorer?'

They each said, 'I do.'

'Amen to that!' Willis looked at Donald. 'The ring!'

'Oh yes!' He produced a ring – a thin gold band with a single stone. Leaning down to

Dolly, he whispered, 'It's a very expensive diamond!' and winked. 'Promise me you'll wear it always. Never take it off your finger. Never – unless I say so.'

'I won't, Don. I promise.'

''Cos you know what they say, don't you? Take off the ring and break the marriage!'

She stared at him, startled. 'I never heard that before.'

'You've never had a wedding ring before!' He slipped it on to her finger.

Grinning, she nodded, knowing that it was glass, but what did she care? It looked wonderful, and she held out her left hand. As she admired the ring, she felt a deep happiness welling up inside her. She was married and that was all she had ever wanted. And expecting a baby. She felt truly blessed and at peace with the world.

Willis said, 'I now declare you husband and wife! Mr and Mrs Donald Wickham!'

Don kissed her, they all shook hands, Willis discreetly accepted payment and blew out the candles.

Don said, 'Right.' In a matter-of-fact way he clapped his hands. 'That's that. All done and dusted! Coming down for a pint of ale, Reverend?'

'Thanks, I will.'

'You won't say no to a drop of gin, will you,

my love?' He slipped his arm through hers.

Dolly nodded and smiled although she felt rather hustled and would have preferred to stay a few moments longer to relish the significance of the ceremony.

Willis gave her an understanding smile and said, 'We must celebrate. This is a very special day, *Mrs Wickham*!'

As Don led his bride from the room, Willis reluctantly took off his 'vestments', folding them carefully and replacing them in an elderly carpet-bag. He folded the green curtains and left them on the table with the candles.

'Oh! The violets!' He snatched them up and, with a last satisfied glance round the room, followed the happy couple down the stairs to the bar.

Three

That evening Dolly stood outside number sixteen, her new home, and stared across the road at number fifteen which from now on would no longer be her home. She was leaving her mother and sister after many shared years. There were tears in her eyes, but she wiped them away, eager to move on and explore her new life as Mrs Donald Wickham on the other side of the road.

She was longing to share the details of her wedding with her mother and Mavis, but she was very anxious about the reception her news would receive when it became clear that they had both missed out on an event which should have been a family occasion followed by a bit of a party. There should have been ale, bread and ham and a cake to be shared by family and friends. They would rightly feel cheated.

Dolly took a deep breath and, avoiding an old man walking with two sticks, and a horse-driven baker's van, she ran lightly across the muddy road and into number fifteen to break the news of her wedding. Letting herself in, she called a greeting and made her way into the kitchen. The small cramped room smelled endearingly of dust and boiled cabbage with overtones of the liniment her mother sometimes needed for her weak hip.

She was expecting her mother's disappointment at being excluded from the ceremony, but was unpleasantly surprised when the news was taken as a personal insult.

'And you never told me, Dolly?' she gasped from the depths of the ancient armchair. 'My own daughter getting married and me not there! Lordy! I can scarce believe it, and that's the truth!' She sank deeper into her chair, her chest heaving with emotion, glaring angrily at Dolly. 'What were you trying to do, young lady – break my bloomin' heart? Well, you've succeeded, and I hope you're satisfied!'

Shocked by this reception, Dolly sat down slowly and regarded her mother speechlessly. May Ellerway had once been pretty, but the years and the efforts of childbearing had taken their toll and her once lithe body was now flabby and her face pasty from too much comfort food. Gin had not helped her body either, but had, on too many occasions, improved her mood. Ten years ago, when her husband died of his liver, she had not bothered to find another man.

Now, thoroughly offended by the news of the wedding, May glared balefully at her youngest daughter.

'There were no guests, Ma,' Dolly argued. 'None at all. It was a small private ceremony. Really small,' she added regretfully. In her heart she still mourned for what she had lost – the music, the presents, the bells ringing and the good wishes. To aggravate her sense of loss, her mother was making her feel like a naughty child being scolded by the teacher. Sidney had given Dolly a drop of gin to bolster her nerves, but it seemed to have lost its potency now that she was face-to-face with her irate mother.

'Ma, I thought you'd be really pleased – because of this!' She patted her belly. 'For the baby's sake and to stop all the gossip. You know what I mean. At least he's made an honest woman of me. I thought that's what you wanted.'

'But getting wed without your own mother? God's truth!' She shook her head. 'And whose idea was this private ceremony? I suppose it's the same wretch who got you into that state! Well, you know what I think of him.'

'You said he was handsome!' Dolly protested. 'A really handsome devil – that's what
you called him.'

'I was being kind, wasn't I! Anyway, looks
aren't everything, and that was ages ago.
He's not bad looking, I suppose, but he's
hardly what you'd call a catch with his back-
ground. Show me trouble and I'll find you a
Wickham mixed up in it somehow!' She
sighed deeply. 'So where was this so-called
"private ceremony"? Which church?'

'It was in a private room.'

Her mother's eyebrows rose. 'So not a
proper religious wedding.'

'Course it was, Ma. Proper and very ... discreet and a bit elegant.' She crossed her
fingers.

'Elegant? What's the point in being elegant
if there was no one there to see it?' May
snorted with derision. 'Elegant, my eye!'

Buffeted into a dismal silence, Dolly glanced down at her clasped hands and was glad
that Mavis was not present to witness her
humiliation.

'So let's see your marriage lines.'

'What?'

'You heard!'

'Marriage lines?'

'The certificate, Doll, what's signed by the
vicar and the best man and everyone. It

proves you were legally married.' Her eyes narrowed. 'Don't tell me you haven't got one!'

The question startled Dolly, but she was at pains to hide the fact. She thought quickly. 'I'm to collect it tomorrow. It ... it has to be copied into the ... Weddings Book.' They must have overlooked it, she assured herself, in their hurry to get down to the bar. Or it might come by post. She would ask Don.

Her mother sat up slowly. 'Jenny Ellerway! If this is all make-believe, just to satisfy me...?'

'Make believe? Course it's not! The Reverend Willis Burke was performing the ceremony – you know – long white robes and everything. Bible, candles...' She sat down, her expression sulky. 'You're never satisfied, Ma! On and on about me being in the family way and no husband and now he's done the decent thing and married me ... Look at this!' She held out the ring Don had given her. 'It's a very expensive diamond. He said so!'

Her mother looked at it and shook her head. 'If that's a diamond I'm Humpty Dumpty!'

'Well, it is!' She wouldn't mention the wink. 'It might be a cheap diamond, but it's really a diam—'

'No such thing as a cheap diamond, you goose! That's glass, that is.'

'You're just jealous!'

Her mother sighed, ignoring the slur. 'I don't know what your sister will say when I tell her!'

On this note the exchange stalled and for a long moment Dolly struggled to defeat the feelings of deflation and insecurity that had rapidly overtaken her. She said, 'The Reverend Burke gave me a bunch of violets as a memento of the wedding. I thought that was really kind of him.'

'They'll be dead in no time.'

'Not if I press them in a book.'

For a moment neither spoke.

'So when's his lordship going to show his face here? Don't I even get to congratulate him?'

'He's over in his place – which is now my place, too – to make it nice for us. Tidy round a bit.'

'I thought he shared the house with his brother.'

'They have their own bedrooms and share the living room.'

Her mother rolled her eyes. 'Let me guess! You're going to skivvy for both of them! Oh Lord. Tell me I'm wrong, for pity's sake.'

'I don't know, and I don't care!'

Heaving herself to her feet, Dolly's mother gave her daughter a peck on the cheek and said, 'That's for good luck. You'll need it! And you won't be getting a wedding present from me, Dolly. Tell him that. Tell him if he couldn't even invite me to my own daughter's wedding...'

But Dolly had had enough cold water poured on her big surprise and, without another word, she turned and fled, slamming the front door behind her.

On Monday morning, Lydia took Adam to the shops to buy him a new pair of shoes. She knew that her husband would be bringing money for the housekeeping, but she didn't want him to find his son looking anything but well kept and in good health. If Don had earned a good sum of money, she might even approach the subject nearest to her heart – which was the possibility of a private school for Adam when he was old enough and, if possible, another baby so that he would not be an 'only child'. Adam would soon be five, and she had her eye on a small private school nearby where she hoped to enrol him. That would leave her alone for weeks on end with no one but her father for company. She secretly craved another child because she had enjoyed motherhood and also believed it would be good for Adam to have a brother or sister to share his life.

George watched them set off to the shops with a pang of regret, but the wind was cool and his daughter had insisted that he should stay in beside the warm fire. As soon as she had closed the front door behind them, George threw down his newspaper and hurried to the front room window to watch their progress along the street.

'Come back soon,' he whispered. He was often irritated by their presence, but he felt bereft the moment they left him and when they had gone from sight there was just him and the grandfather clock which ticked his life away with grim determination. He retrieved *The Times* and smoothed it out, folded it and placed it carefully on the table.

I'll make a pot of tea, he decided and headed for the kitchen where he stood staring round him before stepping outside into the small garden, waiting for inspiration. When none came he went back into the kitchen, but before he could remember why he was there he became aware that someone was knocking at the front door.

'Ah!' He frowned nervously. He waited, holding his breath. Better not to venture out into the hall or he might be spotted by whoever it was. 'Go away!' he muttered. He closed the kitchen door and leaned against it. 'There's no one here.'

The knocking was repeated, and it occurred to him that maybe Lydia had forgotten something and had returned for it. With sudden energy he reopened the kitchen door and rushed along the passage, and he had already opened the door when he realized he had made a mistake. 'Oh!' he gasped.

A complete stranger stood there, a young man, smiling hopefully.

Dismayed, George began to close the door, but then curiosity overcame him. 'What do you want?' he asked. 'I don't know you.'

'Mr Wright sent me.'

'Mr Wright?' George shook his head firmly. 'Wrong address. You've got the wrong address.' He waved a hand to indicate the choice of alternative addresses on either side of the house and added, 'Try one of those.'

The man's smile wavered. 'Mr Wright owns the paper shop. He said—'

'Never heard of the fellow. Now you must excuse me. I'm busy.'

'Aren't you Mr Meecham?'

The door had almost closed, but now George hesitated. He *was* George Meecham. Yes, he was. So how did this young man know that? Unless this was ... His heart leaped at the possibility. He reopened the door.

'Robert? Is it you?'

'No, sir. I'm Leonard Phipps. Mr Wright told me you might have a spare room to let. It wouldn't be permanent. Maybe a few months or at the most a year.'

But George was not listening. He held the door open wide and said, 'Come in! Come in, Robert! This is a surprise. The spare room, you say? But of course.'

'It's Leonard, actually.' The visitor stepped inside, wiping his shoes carefully on the mat and removing his hat. 'This is very kind of you, Mr Meecham. Mr Wright has given you a very good reference.' He laughed, fumbling in his jacket pocket for an envelope. 'This is a reference from my last landlady – my mother, actually – just to let you know I'm an honest and upright citizen. But then she would think so, wouldn't she! I haven't been in lodgings before.'

Pushing the envelope away, George said gruffly, 'No need for that!' and led the way to the kitchen to put on the kettle. 'My daughter Lydia will be home soon,' he told his visitor. 'She's gone to buy the boy some new shoes. My grandson. I forget his name, but you'll like him. Plucky little chap. I'll show you the room while we wait for the kettle.'

Proudly leading the way, he went upstairs, and Leonard Phipps followed. He was a stocky young man with broad shoulders, thick sandy hair and very blue eyes.

'That's the bathroom.' George threw open the door. 'We have had one of the new geysers installed. Don't let it deter you from your weekly bath. A very technical and temperamental machine, but it does produce hot water if it's in a good mood.' He demonstrated. 'You turn on the gas jet – they call it a pilot light, for some reason – and light it and it heats the water in the cylinder above it. Takes a while, but it does work – unless someone opens the bathroom door when a draught might blow out the flames. Can be tricky, but my daughter manages it very well when her husband's away.' He put a finger to his lips. 'Very secret, his work. Something for the government, but I don't enquire.'

'I see. Right.'

George laughed. 'That's my room–' he pointed – 'and that's where the boy sleeps in the small room next to his mother. The spare room which will be yours is up these few steps ... Here we are. Now, what do you think? You'll be very comfortable.'

The room was sparsely furnished, with a large bed on which sat a pile of folded blankets, sheets and two pillows. There was a washstand with a brown and white jug and bowl, a mahogany wardrobe, a chair and

69

table, and chest of drawers which matched the wardrobe. The floor was mainly covered with small rugs placed strategically on the wood floor. The small fireplace boasted a companion set – iron tongs, poker, dustpan and brush – as well as a brass coal scuttle in need of polish.

The young man nodded enthusiastically. 'It's very nice, Mr Meecham. It all rather depends on the price. I do hope we can come to an agreement. I shall be pleased to speak to your daughter about meals and ... and washing facilities.' He gave a discreet glance under the bed to the inevitable china pot.

Seeing this, George said, 'There is a lavatory on the ground floor.'

'I see.'

'There really is no need to consult with my daughter. This is my house, Mr ... What was it?'

'Phipps. Leonard Phipps.'

'Mr Phipps. You can discuss a price with her, however, because there may be a matter of washing clothes and ironing them, cleaning the room, perhaps. We did a lot for poor Miss Baisley.' He frowned. 'If that was her name. I grow forgetful, I'm afraid.' His frown vanished. 'We're a very cheerful family. And you'll like young Adam and my son Robert.' He rubbed his hands with satisfaction. 'I think we shall get along splendidly. Interested in cricket, are you? I used to be a handy all-rounder when I was a young man.'

As the young man followed him down the stairs and attempted to answer, George interrupted him. 'You've been promoted, I believe, hence the move to this area. What exactly do you do, Mr Phipps?'

Mr Phipps' answer came as a pleasant surprise and brought a grin to George's face.

By the time Lydia returned with Adam the two men were discussing the government and its perceived failures. Lydia stared at the young man, who jumped to his feet and began to stammer an explanation of his presence there. 'I have brought a reference,' he told her and took it from his jacket pocket in readiness.

Lydia shook her head, unwilling to accept it.

Adam started to tell him about the shoe shop and his new shoes, which he proudly produced from their box, but Lydia, shocked into silence, now sat down heavily on the sofa and wondered how she could tactfully protest at the arrangement which had been made in her absence.

'My father, I'm sure, had no intention of giving you a firm answer or definitely agreeing to any such plan,' she managed at last, 'and you must understand that I shall have to consult with my husband before we can go ahead.' She turned to her father. 'You knew you should have waited,' she told him.

'I only showed him the room,' he protested. 'There is no need to take this attitude, Liddy.'

'But you have raised poor Mr Phipps' hopes, and that is hardly fair.'

George shrugged his shoulders. 'I simply said that as far as I am concerned the room is his. That is all. If you, or that husband of yours, veto the idea then that is another matter.' He leaned down to Adam. 'What smart shoes your mother has bought for you, but lace-ups? Do you think those small fingers of yours are quite clever enough?'

Leonard Phipps, by this time red-faced with embarrassment, said, 'Oh please, Mrs Daye! I don't want to cause any problems for you. I was not expecting a definite answer today, but simply wanted to know if the room might possibly be suitable and available...' He swallowed. 'I just wanted to know that I need not look any further. I have been granted a day off to arrange my lodgings and open a bank account.'

George, enjoying the situation he had created, had turned his attention to Adam, who was still trying to come to terms with the laces in his new shoes.

Lydia muttered something about 'a pot of tea' and withdrew. Once in the kitchen she rolled her eyes and thought angrily about her father's meddling. As she filled the tea-pot, however, she thought about Leonard Phipps, who seemed a nice enough man with good manners – but what on earth would John say? Very likely he would see the other man as an interloper and would immediately veto the idea of accepting him as a lodger, which would be difficult after her father had almost promised him the room.

She sighed as she set the tea tray with three cups and saucers. John would probably pro-test that they had no need of extra money as his own work provided for them very com-fortably, which was true, but the idea of someone else living in the house while John was away was now, after some thought, be-coming quite appealing. If, as had happened several times, her father wandered off, there would be two people to go in search of him instead of one.

An hour later that same day, when John arrived home Lydia met him in the hall. He kissed his wife and hugged his son and Lydia opened her mouth to begin the little speech she had rehearsed about the presence of Leonard Phipps and the possibility of him becoming a lodger. However, her father forestalled her as they entered the room where Leonard Phipps was still waiting to know his fate.

George said, 'Hullo again, John. Meet Mr Phipps who is going to be our new lodger. You'll like him. Very solid sort of chap. Has to be. He's a policeman.'

Four

When Dolly came downstairs on Monday morning she found Sidney alone at the breakfast table with a basin of beef dripping which he was spreading on to a thick slice of bread cut from a large cob loaf. There was no sign of Don.

Sidney glanced up, chewing furiously, swallowed and said, 'He said to tell you he loves you and he's had to rush to get some stuff up to Manchester on the train.'

Her jaw dropped. 'What? Already? He was away yesterday and all!'

'Don't give me that look, Dolly. You can't blame me.'

'You mean he's gone off without even telling me? Gone back to work?'

'Got it in one!'

'For how long? I mean, is he coming back today?'

'Might. Might not.' He indicated the bread. 'Help yourself.'

She shook her head. 'But we was only wed

75

Saturday!'

'You've got a good memory.' He pretended not to notice the quiver in her voice. 'Don't worry. He'll be back. Like a bad penny, our Don. Don't you want any breakfast? Beef dripping.' He indicated the basin. 'Tasty, that is.'

She sat down reluctantly. 'I like marmalade.'

'Shame we haven't got any.' He took another large mouthful.

After a moment she gave him a coy smile. 'Hope we didn't keep you awake last night!'

'I'm used to it.'

'What?' She stared at him. 'Used to it? You mean he...'

'You weren't the first woman in his life, Dolly. Be sensible.' He washed his bread and dripping down with a mouthful of tea. 'And just lately you two were up to it most lunchtimes if I remember rightly. Bed springs going nineteen to the dozen!'

Dolly said, 'You shouldn't have been listening!'

'You made enough noise!' He helped himself to another spoonful of sugar and stirred the tea vigorously.

Dolly said, 'Or porridge. Got any porridge oats?'

'No.'

She gave an exaggerated sigh and poured herself a cup of tea.

'So, what's it like being married, Mrs Wickham?'

She shrugged. 'Don't know, really. I mean, nothing's very different. I've fallen out with me ma, but that's Don's fault for not letting her come to the wedding.' She gave him a long look. 'You didn't turn up either.'

'My guts were playing up something chronic.'

Dolly pursed her lips, disapproving of the way the conversation was going. 'How is it that Don works so hard and is away so often and you're always hanging about here doing nothing?'

He gave the question earnest consideration. 'I help him out from time to time.'

'You?' She tossed her head at the very idea. 'When do you help him out? You're not a salesman.'

'He has certain jobs that need a partner. Certain important jobs. Then it's me. Me and him.'

'Pull the other leg. It's got bells on!'

'OK then. Me, I've got a private income,' he said, grinning. 'Family money. My grandfather left me money.'

Dolly's eyes widened. 'He left you money? Just you? What about Don?'

77

For a moment he hesitated. 'He lived with us, but he never liked Don even though he was better looking when he was a kid. Grandpa was a cantankerous old sod, but I was his favourite. I was named after him, and he liked that. Sidney Archibald Wickham. That was his name. Proper old money-bags, he was.'

'Well, I think that was really mean. Two brothers, and he only left money for one.' She broke a piece of crust from the loaf and nibbled it absent-mindedly. 'I don't think I'd have liked a man like that. Having favourites. Poor Don.'

'Don was a bit of a brat, that's why. Always dodging off school or getting the cane. Always answering back. I'd like a pound for every time he got a clout round the ear from someone. Used to throw clods of earth at the old man's cat just to annoy him. He had this mangy old tabby – it must have been a hundred in cat years – but the old man adored it. Lord knows why!'

'So are you rich?'

'From time to time!' He laughed. 'Maybe you picked the wrong brother!'

'I feel rich. Look!' She held out her left hand and waggled her fingers. 'My ma says it's glass, but what does she know about anything? I think it's—'

To her surprise Sidney grabbed at her hand and eyed the ring through narrowed eyes. 'When did he give you this? When *exactly* did he give you this?'

'It's my wedding ring. Don forgot to buy a gold band so he gave me this instead.' With an effort she snatched her hand from his grasp. 'At least he worked for it. It wasn't just handed to him on a plate by his grandfather!'

Sidney was staring at her as if he had seen a ghost. 'When did he give you that ring?' he repeated.

'I told you. Saturday.' She could almost see his brain working – thoughts whirling round in his head.

He leaned forward suddenly. 'Want to know if it's real? I mean, he might have palmed you off with glass, like your ma said. I know a chap who could tell you the truth. He's an expert, this chap. But you'd have to let me take it to him.'

'I'd better not.'

'He won't know.'

'I'm not supposed to take it off. Not ever.' She was weakening. How wonderful to have it approved by an expert! She would tell her mother. That would put her nose out of joint and serve her right.

'So what do you say?' he asked.

She hesitated. 'I don't know. He might find out. I'll think about it. How's that?'

'Not much to think about, is there? Either he lied to you or he didn't.' He leaned closer. 'Either he's taken you for a fool or he hasn't!' He pushed back his chair. 'Well, I'm off. Don't forget to do the washing up!'

Dolly blinked, outraged for a moment, but then she rallied. 'And where are you off to in such a hurry if you don't work?'

He put a finger to his lips. 'Wild horses wouldn't drag it out of me!' he told her. He reached for a jacket from the hooks behind the door, punched his arms into the sleeves, wiped the remains of his breakfast from his mouth with the back of his hand and was gone, slamming the door behind him.

Dolly sat there for a long time, struggling with her feelings. On the one hand she was now a married woman and ought to feel happy, but on the other hand her husband had disappeared. She felt neglected and wanted to run home for a cup of tea and one of her mother's rock cakes, but that was out of the question. Her mother would gloat. As for doing the washing up! She stared round her. That would be skivvying, wouldn't it?

She wondered what her sister Mavis would think of missing the wedding. No doubt she would also be annoyed. Jealous, too. Dolly smiled. Then her smile faded. Ma would tell Mavis that there were no marriage lines.

Maybe she should go back to Clarence Street to the Rose and Garter, ask them where the reverend lived and then collect the marriage lines.

She was still undecided when the postman arrived and handed her a couple of letters. One was for a Mr John Daye.

She ran after the postman, waving the envelope. 'You've given me the wrong letter,' she told him breathlessly. 'No one of that name lives at number sixteen. I know because I live there now I'm married!' She waited for his congratulations. 'Saturday,' she elaborated. 'Don't you recognize me? I used to live opposite.' She pointed helpfully.

He handed it back. 'It says number sixteen, Mansoor Street. That's where I deliver it. There must be an office on the top floor. See?' He ran a finger under the address. 'PSD. Third Floor.'

'But it must be a mistake,' she insisted. 'There's only the ground floor and the first floor where the bedrooms are – unless the third floor means the attic. Anyway, what does PSD stand for?'

'Don't rightly know and don't care. Not my job, miss, to know everything. I just deliver the letters.'

'It's not "Miss", it's *"Mrs"*. I told you. I'm married. Mrs Donald Wickham.' She smiled, suddenly cheerful again. 'We were wed Saturday. A private ceremony!'

'Well, that's as may be, but that letter stays where I delivered it. Most likely it's one of those special drop-off places where a firm doesn't have shop or an office but has an address so people can write to them.' He thrust the envelope into her hand again and walked quickly away before she could delay him further.

Dolly went back into the house, slightly crushed by his lack of interest in her marriage, and propped the letter behind the clock on the narrow mantelpiece. The other letter was addressed to Sidney and looked like a bill of some kind. Her mother dreaded bills, but presumably Sidney wouldn't worry because he had family money and was rich.

'PSD?' she muttered. 'Private Shop? No–o ... Personal Service Delivery! Something like that. Anyway, what *is* in the attic?' Dust usually, she thought. A 'drop-off place'? She had a lot to learn. Moving towards the sink she put the plug in and added cold water and what was left in the kettle. She found a cloth and rubbed some soap into the water and frothed it up. She began to wash up because there was nothing else to do. She had put the violets on her bedroom window for Don to admire, and she would press them in a day or two. She would buy a scrap book and write things in it like the day the baby was born ... or what happened when they went to Ramsgate for the day. Don had promised her the latter by way of a honeymoon, but not just yet because he was so busy at work.

She sighed. In her old life she would have been at work behind the counter in the bakery on the corner, chatting cheerfully to the familiar customers. Mrs Braggs coming in for her two sausage rolls for their lunch; Miss Warren from the end house buying a stale bun to toast for her tea; young Jimmy Stokes with a penny pocket money for an apricot jam tart. Dolly knew them all and served them with genuine pleasure.

Except on Saturdays, of course, when she and Mavis would have wandered round the market, eating toffee apples, or maybe buying a new ribbon for a hat, chatting with friends and exchanging their news. But now they were married Don had said he was a 'man of means' and she could give up work, what with the baby coming and everything, and he didn't want her out with her girlfriends all the time, 'tittle-tattling' about her private life.

For a moment she felt lonely, mourning the passing of that part of her life. She was almost tempted to go in search of her friends, but reluctantly reminded herself how eager she had been for change. Her friends would envy her the fact that she now had a husband and would soon have a baby to care for. No, she decided. She must forgo the delights of the market and would wait in dutifully because her husband might come back sooner than later.

'Skivvying!' she whispered, but she was a married woman after all, and suppose her mother relented and decided to pop across and see how she was getting on? The kitchen looked a mess. Glancing round she saw that the floor was littered with crumbs and what looked like sawdust. Later on she would sweep up, she decided. Don would be pleasantly surprised when he came back.

Not a mile away Leonard Phipps was writing to his mother in far away Bedfordshire. He sat in his rented room over the bar in the Merry Monarch and pencilled the words into a large notebook supplied by the Metropolitan Police and intended to receive information on crimes. He didn't think they would miss one or two pages.

 ... So you see, I shall be very comfortable in my

new room with the Dayes and well fed in the evening (sixpence per hot dinner) and will sleep well on the bed, which has a good horsehair mattress.

Mrs Daye has promised a scuttle full of coal when the weather is cold and has sent for the sweep as she has found a few feathers in the grate and thinks a bird has nested in the chimney...

Leonard sharpened his pencil and continued.

Her husband, who is away on business a lot, seems a decent sort and made no bones about me having the room. Old Mr Meecham is very vague and several times called me Robert, but that is no problem, and little Adam seems a nice child and well behaved.

Work is going well – we hear plenty of gossip about the rest of London including that recent robbery by jewel thieves in London during which a man was knocked down. It seems he is not expected to survive so we may soon all be involved in a hunt for a killer! That would be useful experience.

So far, dearest mother, I have not stumbled into any 'dens of vice', nor have I been corrupted in any way!

I shall move in to my new room on Monday and will write to you again next week. Don't worry about me. All is well. Yours truly, Lennie.

He tore the sheet from the notebook and

folded it, then slipped it into an envelope and carefully addressed it. His widowed mother, country born and bred, had dreaded his move to London, but he had insisted that the move was his only chance of early promotion.

Already, he had seen more action on the beat in one day than he had in the village in a week. Gleefully, he counted them on the fingers of one hand – a street fight outside a pub in the morning, an accident involving a horse and cart and a motor car which resulted in broken headlamps, large-scale thefts of fruit from the Billingsgate market reported in the afternoon and a burglary from a church collection box discovered just before evensong.

At home in Bedfordshire he had spent most of his time on his bicycle, chasing groups of speeding cyclists. He grinned at the memories. He'd seen enough 'scorchers' to last him a lifetime and had put up with quite enough back answers from them.

Although he was now on foot he found his beat an exciting place, but he would always dilute it for his mother's benefit. Murderous gangs would become rowdy groups, a raid on a local shop would become young thieves and a stolen horse would become a runaway animal. Nor would he mention the bullying

86

Sergeant O'Malley, or the uniform which did not fit as well as it might so the back of the collar rubbed his neck. His mother had been born to worry, and he wanted to spare her the anxiety of thoughts of her precious son floundering in the well-reported wickedness of London streets. Life was never perfect, he told himself, and for the moment he was well satisfied with his lot.

That night, as the church clock struck midnight, John lay wide awake, his arm round his sleeping wife. Lydia was snoring faintly in a feminine way which always touched his heart. The moonlight revealed her hair, dishevelled on the pillow, and he knew that her often anxious face, now softened by sleep, would look much younger. Only a few years older than Dolly, he thought, with a deep feeling of guilt. Poor Dolly would be sleeping alone, the first of many such nights. He sighed. She would have to get used to it. At least he had given her the appearance of respectability she had craved.

Lydia stirred in her sleep and turned over and away from him without waking. He tucked himself round her sleeping form and wished that he had managed his life better. Women were such a trial – so tempting, so very needful. Knowing that a man loved them was never enough, somehow. At least he and Lydia were legally married – apart from the false name he had used. He had done that much for her, and he tried to take comfort from the thought.

At the time he had wanted a family, believing that was the way to put down roots; believing that he wanted to change his life-style; believing that with the right support he could become a better person. What a fool he had been, and how hopelessly naive to imagine that he and Sidney could rise above their beginnings. Not that they were without resources, but money wasn't everything, and Lydia's father had immediately known him for what he was. 'A jumped up Jack' was the phrase he had once used in an attempt to dissuade Lydia from marrying him. Although George Meecham had no idea of the extent of his son-in-law's wrongdoings, he had recognized him for what he wasn't. John Daye was not a decent man, and he was not the sort of man a father would approve of for a son-in-law.

If he, John, had a daughter of his own he would never allow her to associate with a man like him, but by the time George had got some measure of his son-in-law's serious shortcomings the old man was becoming disorientated and unable to convince Lydia of her true predicament.

John sighed. The year was rushing past him. It was already May – outside, a more than frisky wind rushed through the newly green trees – and his life was still precarious. He wanted something to change, but he didn't know how. He wanted to be a good husband and father, but in his line of business it was difficult. Falling for sweet little Dolly had made it worse, of course. He should have had more sense. A soft groan escaped him. No right-minded thief could expect to enjoy a settled life, and he was no exception.

Listening to the gusts outside their window, he tried to go back to sleep but, as usual, his mind was too active, and he knew he would lie sleepless for hours, racked by regrets and full of doubts for the future.

Lydia sighed deeply and suddenly woke up and turned over. 'Are you awake, John?'

'Yes.'

'I'm glad you're back. I always fear for you when you're away. Father insists that you are sometimes in danger.'

'I'm not. But if I were, I can take care of myself.'

'Where were you this time?'

'You're not supposed to ask. I've explained.'

'But if you give me a clue and I *guess*, then you haven't really told me anything.' She turned back towards him and tried to study his face in the light from the window.

'It starts with E,' he said wearily, knowing how persistent she could be.

'England!'

'No.'

'Estonia.'

He shook his head. 'Much nearer home.'

A long pause. 'Ethiopia!'

'Ethiopia? That's not nearer home. Anyway, it's not a country, it's a town.'

'Ethiopia is a *town*?' she queried.

'No! Where I've been to is a town!' He tried to keep the exasperation from his voice.

'I give up, then,' she told him.

'Aberdeen.'

Raising herself on one elbow she stared into his face, trying to make out his expression in the dim light. 'Aberdeen? You said it started with E!'

'Did I say Aberdeen?' He cursed silently. He was getting careless. 'Sorry, dearest. My mistake. I meant Edinburgh.' He hugged her. 'So you see I was never far away. You worry too much.'

'Anyway, I *said* England!'

'Edinburgh is in Scotland.'

'Oh yes, of course.'

They lay silent for a while.

Lydia said, 'I'm glad you agreed to let Mr Phipps stay here. I think it will be good for Father as well as Adam. Especially as he's a policeman. He must be a very upright sort of man. Trustworthy, don't you think? Maybe a trifle dull.'

'I would hope so.' He rolled his eyes, unseen. A policeman was the last person he would have chosen as a lodger, but when confronted with a *fait accompli* he had been unable to think fast enough. 'And don't you get any ideas about him, Lydia, or let him get ideas about you. I wouldn't like to have to fight a duel over you – I might lose!' He laughed, but there was a hollow ring to the words. He had fought before, in his youth, and had never lost.

'Get ideas about Mr Phipps? Good heavens, no!' Lydia kissed him. 'I like my men exciting and mysterious, like you. Anyway, he's probably promised to a young lady back home in Bedfordshire.'

Best place for a young lady, John thought wryly. Keep the women at arm's-length. That's what he himself should have done. He should have sent Dolly packing before things went too far, but the baby had complicated matters and she had threatened to throw herself off Blackfriars Bridge into the

Thames if he deserted her. Now the best he could hope for was to keep the two women apart. So far he'd been rather good at that, but there was 'many a slip between cup and lip', as they said, and he worried about his brother. Sidney was hardly the brightest card in the pack, and expecting him to keep a secret – *any* secret – was fraught with risk. One day their luck would run out.

'At least,' she said sleepily, 'we'll be safe with a policeman in the house – if we were to be burgled or anything.'

'That's a comforting thought,' he murmured. 'Now go back to sleep, Lydia. It will be time to get up before we know it.'

'Can you stay until Sunday? We could go to church together. I'd like that.'

And I could confess my sins, he thought, his amusement tinged with bitterness. 'Sorry, dearest, but no. You know how much I hate all that singing and chanting. If I'm still here we'll go to the Saturday Market instead, and I'll buy you a new hat and a toy for Adam. Maybe a cigar for me.'

As she settled happily against him he drew in a deep breath. And never a thought for tomorrow, he reminded himself. In his view, tomorrows could not be trusted. He had always preferred to live for the moment and take his chances.

★ ★ ★

Next day Dolly's sister Mavis arrived at number sixteen just as Dolly had finished her efforts in the kitchen and was admiring the results. The sink was empty of dirty plates, and the once grimy saucepan had been hung on a convenient hook on the wall. The kitchen table had been swept free of stale crumbs, and a variety of clothes, casually draped over the few chairs, had been banished to a row of hooks on the back of the door that led out on to the small yard in which a newly washed tea towel was drying in the wind.

When Dolly found her sister waiting on the doorstep she threw her arms around her and then, remembering her elevated status as a married woman, invited her in, apologizing as she led the way back to the kitchen for the fact that the wedding had been private.

Mavis, two years older than Dolly, was not easily mollified. With a dismissive shrug, she said, 'Sounds as if I didn't miss much. Ma says it was a miserable affair with no hymns and stuff.'

Mavis, shorter and with a well-rounded body, was less attractive than her sister, but had once had an admirer who subsequently abandoned her for someone younger. This unkind treatment had left its mark on her face by way of a disagreeable expression, though this was occasionally relieved by a smile which surprised people.

Dolly was trying to hide her hurt feelings. 'It wasn't miserable! It was sort of elegant. A very simple ceremony, but ... touching.' She led the way into the newly cleaned kitchen where Mavis remained standing, glancing round without comment. Dolly ploughed on with her defence of the wedding. 'I sometimes think too many people spoil things.'

'No, they don't. I shall invite lots of people to *my* wedding.'

Dolly, recognizing a hint of 'sour grapes', bit back an obvious rejoinder.

Mavis was now frowning. Dolly rushed to defend her kitchen. 'Just big enough,' she said. 'Like ours back home. Those big kitchens people have – you'd get worn out rushing round in them. This is convenient.' She swallowed. 'So is Ma still mad at me?'

'You know Ma! She likes to bear a grudge, but she'll be all right when the baby comes. She's always wanted to be a grandmother.' Mavis stood in front of the shelves, which held a motley assortment of crockery, and came across the letter which the postman had insisted on delivering. Taking it down, she stared at the address. 'PSD Third Floor. What's that then?'

'I dunno.'

'You should. You live here.'

'Only since yesterday. The third floor must be some sort of attic. A sort of office, I suppose.'

'Who's Mr John Daye?' She held the envelope up to the light, squinting, trying to glimpse a shape of the contents.

'Don't know. Don't care.' Dolly was becoming irritated. She wanted her sister to be impressed, to envy her her married state – not to ask stupid questions. To change the subject she said, 'Don's brother is decent enough. It's fun having a brother-in-law.'

'Sidney? Ma says he's a layabout.'

'He's got time on his hands because he's got private money so he doesn't have to have a job.' Seeing that the information had caught her sister's interest, she added, 'Maybe you could marry him and be my sister-in-law.'

Mavis thought about it. 'How could I? I'm already your sister. Anyway, his eyes are too close together.'

'He can't help that. He's got a nice voice.'

Mavis laughed. 'Can you imagine what Ma would say? It's bad enough *you* marrying a Wickham! If we both did it she'd be tearing her hair out!' Before Dolly could decide to take offence at this slur on her husband,

Mavis quickly changed the subject. 'We could steam it open. The letter, I mean.'

'Certainly not!'

'Why? You're a married woman now, Doll – you can do what you like.'

'It belongs to someone upstairs.'

Mavis gave a fiendish grin. 'Let's take it up to them, whoever they are. If there's nobody there and it's not locked we can have a look round the office, and if it's locked we can push the letter under the door. Really, Dolly, I can't believe you've never been up there.'

'I didn't live here then, did I? Don said they had nothing to do with the "upstairs lot" ... and I'm not the nosy type.'

'You always were!'

Dolly ignored the remark. It was true that she *was* a married woman, so presumably she could do more or less what she liked. Without a word she led the way up the stairs, along the landing and up a few steps at the end of the passage where they were met by a flimsy-looking door with peeling paint.

Mavis leaned past Dolly and rapped on the door.

Nothing.

Dolly said, 'I've never heard footsteps overhead. Perhaps they only open the office on certain days – like Mondays, Wednesdays and Fridays.' She turned the handle. To their surprise the door creaked open, and after a moment's hesitation they pushed inside the room, squashed together as they went through the narrow opening.

It was a surprisingly bleak and disappointing sight – a large empty room, smelling musty and damp, and lit at the far end by a small, very dirty window. The low angled ceiling was hung with cobwebs and twisted strips of what Dolly assumed had once been ceiling paper.

'Ugh!' said Dolly and took a small step backwards.

There was a somewhat ramshackle table in one corner on which a small chest stood in solitary splendour among old faded newspapers and a sprinkling of sawdust. Two stools completed the furniture. Dolly shivered with distaste, but Mavis hurried forward and tried to open the chest.

'It's locked.' Her dismay was evident.

'Don't touch it!' cried Dolly. 'It's nothing to do with us.'

'It's nothing to do with anyone, if you ask me. This isn't an office, it's an empty attic.' Mavis shook the box close to her ear. 'I think it's buried treasure!' she grinned. 'It rattles.'

'It's hardly *buried*!' Looking around her, Dolly frowned. 'You're right, for once. You couldn't call this an office, could you, unless it was once an office but it's closed down and people don't know and still keep sending letters and getting no answer.'

'So we could go downstairs and open the letter ... maybe answer it.'

'Mavis! That's a terrible idea ... but I suppose we could.' She sighed. 'Better not, though. Don might be angry.'

'Not if I did it. Anyway, how would he know? We could stick the flap down again.'

'I said no!'

'Hoity toity!'

Dolly had crossed the room and now peered out of the window on to the street below. 'Strange to see my old home from somewhere else – from my married home.' Sighing, she turned. 'Does Ma know you're here?'

'It was her idea. She said, "Get over there and see if she's all right" – meaning you.'

So her mother still cared about her. Dolly hid her relief.

An hour later, when her sister had gone and neither of the brothers had returned, Dolly put her reservations aside, put on the kettle and steamed open the envelope.

Five

When the postman called three days later in Parmettor Street he delivered a letter for Lydia which she could not understand and which came from someone she had never heard of. After reading it through several times she wondered whether to share it with her father, but decided against it. There was no reason he should understand it, and it might prey on his mind. John was away again on business so she could not discuss it with him, either. That evening, however, when Leonard Phipps came down for his evening meal, she thought she would seek a reaction from him.

'It's come from a Mrs Wickham,' she told him as she carried a bowl of mashed potatoes to the table and followed it with a dish of beef stew with onions.

George drew up a chair, and Leonard helped Adam on to his chair, which boasted a cushion to give him extra height at the table.

The boy eyed the beef nervously. 'Is there gristle, Mama?' he asked.

George said, 'Gristle? You must not fuss over a piece of gristle, Adam. It won't hurt you. When I was your age I used to just shut my eyes and swallow it down. You do that, Adam, and you won't worry about gristle ever again.'

Leonard Phipps said, 'A letter from a stranger? How very odd. I'll read it when I've finished my dinner. It smells delicious.' He turned to George. 'My mother says you can't beat the smell of nicely cooked beef.'

'Beef is good, Mr Phipps, I grant you, but for me it's a mutton stew. Plenty of carrots and onions ... or a pie.' He nodded. 'Yes, maybe that was it. A nice mutton pie.'

Lydia leaned down to her son and said softly, 'I won't give you any gristle, Adam. Don't worry.' As they helped themselves to the beef and vegetables she said, 'The strangest part is that this woman – a Mrs Donald Wickham – also enclosed one of my letters to my husband saying that the office of PSD has closed down. I'm sure if it had done John would have told me.'

Leonard said, 'So presumably he hasn't read your letter. He'll be disappointed, no doubt.'

Adam took a mouthful of meat, closed his

eyes and swallowed.

George laughed. 'Slips right down!' he cried. 'What did I tell you, Adam?' He tapped the side of his nose. 'You listen to your grandpapa, young man, and you won't go far wrong!'

Lydia began to relax. During the day, her father had not referred once to Robert, which she always looked upon as a good sign, and she was secretly hopeful that he would somehow make a startling and unexpected recovery. He certainly seemed more genial when Leonard Phipps was around.

Now George said, 'The papers are still reporting the robbery at Glazers. Are you hearing anything on the grapevine, Mr Phipps?'

'We are, yes. I fear the whole thing has turned rather unpleasant. The chap who was knocked unconscious has taken a turn for the worse and we expect he won't survive much longer. We do have a witness, though, and we also have a very vague artist's sketch of one of the perpetrators. It's not very precise, but a man was waiting in a car outside when the raid started and our witness caught a glimpse of one of them as the other two pushed their way in, shouting and causing a panic.'

'Shouting what, exactly?' Lydia asked.

'"Put up your hands!"' He shrugged. 'Not very original, was it? I suspect they had not planned that part of the raid in much detail.'

She shook her head. 'And in broad daylight, too! How do they dare to try it? You would imagine that the chances against them succeeding were huge.'

Leonard shrugged. 'There are people who will stop at nothing. They seem to disregard the risks. Maybe they enjoy the thrill of the theft itself and also the excitement of a possible chase. Not to mention the satisfaction they must feel when – *if* – they succeed.'

'As these bounders did!' George pursed his lips. 'Would you assume that they have done it before? And got away unscathed?'

Leonard nodded. 'We think they are professional thieves. Beginners would never have started with a big London store.'

Lydia said, 'That would be foolhardy in the extreme.'

Leonard refilled his water glass. 'Of course, all the jewellers are now on high alert, but they'll forget as time passes. The witness says the two men rushed out of the shop and scrambled into the car and one of them shouted, "Go, Will!"' He grinned. 'Broke two of the golden rules. Don't let anyone hear your voice and don't use names! We conclude that the one who called out was a

Londoner and the driver was called Will!'

Lydia frowned. 'So his name must have been William Somebody. A useful clue, isn't it?'

Her father laughed. 'Hardly! Think how many Williams there must be in London!'

Leonard smiled at her. 'But you're right, Mrs Daye. It's better than nothing.'

She nodded. 'And now the poor man who was knocked down may die?'

'Yes. It was probably an accident, but he's still in a critical condition. Same method as the last two – rush in, terrify them, snatch whatever's within reach and scarper! London accents, so most likely local men rather than a gang from, say, Manchester. Stolen car, later abandoned in a brewer's yard in Peckham.'

George said, 'I had a son, but he's ... I suppose he's grown up now. Don't see much of him. Robert, I mean.' He looked at Lydia and lowered his voice. 'Or is he dead?'

'He died a good few years ago, Father,' she reminded him gently.

'Ah! I thought as much ... but he was called Robert, not William. You're getting a bit mixed up, dear.' He turned to Leonard. 'I keep an eye open for him, Mr Phipps. You never know, do you? Not these days.'

'No–o. I suppose not.'

103

Adam said, 'Is it trifle, Mama? Or rice pudding?'

'It's trifle, Adam,' she told him, grateful for the interruption. 'And what a nice clean plate! You've eaten all your dinner.'

George smiled proudly. 'You see that, Mr Phipps? The boy's got a good appetite.'

Later that evening George retired to bed early, and Lydia found herself alone with Leonard Phipps.

When the church clock struck nine he said, 'I'm on an early shift tomorrow so I'd best get some sleep. Did you want me to have a look at your mysterious letter before I go up?'

'If you would be so kind,' she replied eagerly. 'I'm probably making much ado about nothing, but it does seem odd.'

She handed it to him, and he read it silently:

Dear Lydia, I fownd yor letter in the atic of my home (Im newly wed) and you shoud know the office of PSD is closed so the letter will not reech yor husband. Yors truly, Mrs Donald Wickham.

He handed back the letter, and Lydia regarded him uneasily. 'I suppose my husband forgot to mention it.'

'You'll no doubt mention it to him when he next comes home – which will be when, exactly?'

'That's it. I never know. He is rarely able to let me know in advance, but I shall show him the letter, certainly.'

'This Mrs Wickham is obviously not a secretary – her spelling shows that – but if she is recently married and has moved into number sixteen she must know what she is talking about. What does your husband actually do, Mrs Daye?'

Lydia hesitated. 'I'm not allowed to discuss it, but I can say he works for the government on ... on secret business. He travels for them and is often away for days at a time. Sometimes weeks.' Seeing that he was not satisfied, she tried to elaborate. 'I think it's to do with documents that they can't trust to the postal system.'

'Like a courier? Is that what you mean?'

'If that's what couriers do, then yes. John says it's safer that I don't know too much because then I can't accidentally let anything slip.'

'Hm.' He frowned. 'So where does he live when he's not here?'

'I don't know. I don't need to know, you see. Hotels, I suppose. Sometimes his business takes him abroad. That address in Mansoor Street was always the place where he could collect my letters to him.' She smiled.

'It all sounds very important.'

'I believe it is. I'm rather proud of him, to tell you the truth.'

'You must be. You seem to deal with it very well, but it must be lonely for you.'

Lydia shrugged. 'I'm used to it – and there's Adam and Father. I miss John, naturally, but I can't claim to be lonely. Not that Father is good company, but I can't blame him for his condition. He must be very confused much of the time, and I try to keep his memory as clear as I can.'

'If it's not too personal a question, may I ask what happened to your brother Robert?'

She hesitated. 'My brother was killed in a road accident. He was only thirteen. I was ten and I worshipped him. I'm sure he found me a nuisance, but he loomed large in my little world. For a long time they were afraid to tell me he was dead so I kept waiting for him to come home from the hospital.'

'That must have been terrible for you. I'm so sorry.'

Lydia sighed. 'Two vehicles collided in the street. One was a hackney carriage, and the horse reared up and somehow slipped its traces and raced through the crowd on the pavement.' She swallowed hard. 'It trampled several people including Robert, who died a few weeks later in hospital. My mother maintained that it broke my father's heart and was the beginning of his ... difficulties.'

'What a nightmare! I shouldn't have asked for details. It was thoughtless of me. Do please forgive me, Mrs Daye.'

She took several deep breaths.

To change the subject, Leonard said, 'So your husband is not a spy!'

She gave a shaky laugh. 'Quite the opposite, in fact. A very upright citizen, in fact. Father likes to tease me. It seems to amuse him, and I can put up with it most of the time – but, of course, I don't like Adam to hear it. He adores his father.' She glanced at the clock. 'But look at the time! And you have an early start in the morning. I hope the weather improves for you.'

'So do I. Early-morning fog is what I hate most. Yesterday it was a real pea-souper! My mother swears that it gets into the lungs. "London lungs", she calls it, like a disease, because of all the soot and smoke in the air.'

'My husband thinks London is the dirtiest city in the world.'

'I dare say if he travels a lot he can make a judgement.'

They made their 'goodnights' and Lydia watched him as he went up the stairs. As lodgers go, she thought, Leonard Phipps is a pleasant person to have about the house.

Next morning at number sixteen Don and Sidney ate their bread and dripping in an uneasy silence until Don said, 'Out with it!'

'That ring!' Sidney had been trying to pluck up the courage to air his grievance. 'You hung on to it. You said you'd got rid of it all and divvied up the money.'

'So I did. Who says I didn't?'

'I do. I've got eyes in my head. The ring you gave to Dolly.'

'It's glass, you idiot.'

'You're lying, Don. You're a cheat and a liar!'

'Watch your mouth, Sid, or I might just punch it!'

'It's a diamond,' cried Sidney, red-faced with anger. 'I'm not as daft as I look. It's your way of keeping a bit extra for yourself. I'm wise to you now, Don. I thought something was adrift last time, but I couldn't prove it. I knew I couldn't trust you! Now I'm sure.'

'Last time? What happened last time?' Don sprinkled pepper and salt on to his bread and dripping, counting to ten inside his head and hoping he had not been rumbled. He had always kept back a small amount to satisfy himself for being the brains of the business. He could not do the jobs alone so

Sid was a necessary accomplice, but he, Don, planned the operations and sold on the goods.

'What happened?' Sidney glared at him. 'You told me those pearls were second-rate, but I spotted them in a shop in Chelsea. I recognized that clasp.'

Don stopped eating and leaned forward until their noses were almost touching. 'It's glass!' he repeated slowly and emphatically.

'What? Glass?' He looked confused, as Don had intended.

'The ring. The so-called diamond. It's *glass*.'

'I'm talking about the pearls – about last time.'

Don sat back. 'If you saw those pearls on sale for top whack then Jimmy Fisk has cheated me. You should have told me.' He tried to look aggrieved. 'Bit late now. Can't prove anything. They'll be long gone.' He sighed heavily. Glancing at his brother he saw the doubt he had hoped to provoke and took his chance. 'As for the ring, you can take it to a jeweller. Don't shake your head! I want you to. Set your mind at ease. Take it to Arnie Harrold. He'll tell you what it is.' He held his breath, crossing the fingers of his left hand beneath the table. Arnie Harrold was a fence, and what he did not know about precious stones was not worth knowing. 'But don't tell Dolly!' he added. 'She thinks it's real, bless her.'

'I'd have to tell her to get hold of the ring.'

'Just say you want to know how much I paid for it!' He was thinking on his feet now, praying that he could convince his brother of his honesty. 'Tell her not to tell me you've asked to borrow it.' He sighed. 'You are so suspicious, Sid! After all these years, and you still don't trust me. I suppose it's just in your nature.'

Sidney wavered. 'What about the other one? Lydia.'

Don's heart sank. 'Lydia? What about her?'

'Have you given her one? I bet you have. I bet you've given them both a diamond ring! You thieving bugger!' He sprang to his feet and glared down at Don. 'So you owe me, Don Wickham. Whatever those rings are worth you owe me the same!'

'I owe you nothing, Sid.' He spoke regretfully, as if to a child. 'I've told you, the ring is glass. Ask her. You have my permission.' He held out both hands in a helpless gesture. 'What have I got to lose? Take the ring and check it out with Arnie, and then let's hear your apology!' He saw the indecision in his brother's eyes. He told himself he was almost there. 'And I haven't given Lydia anything you don't know about. You have the answer, Sid. You've always had the answer. You can walk away from it all.'

'You need me!'

'I don't. It's you that needs me! We've done very nicely for ourselves all these years, but if you want to go it alone, suits me.'

He stood up, and at that moment the front door opened and Dolly came in, breathless and beaming, with a basket full of food from the market. 'I've got a nice bit of 'addock...' she began, but then noticed the tension in the air. 'What?' she asked. 'Something happened?'

Sidney stared at her for a moment, opened and closed his mouth, and then pushed past her and left the room without a word.

Don grinned. 'Only Sid in one of his moods. He'll get over it. I think he's jealous. I told him, "Find a woman of your own!"'

She smiled, setting down the basket on the kitchen table. 'My sister's not spoken for,' she told him.

He laughed. 'He's seen your sister!'

Dolly gasped, then laughed. She pretended to cuff him round the ear, but allowed him to catch her wrist and pull her down on to his lap. 'You're a wicked man, Don Wickham!' she said as his arms closed around her. Catching sight of her ring she held it out to

111

admire it.

Don said, 'Remember what I said, won't you – never take it off. Not for anyone. Understand?'

'As if I would!'

'Promise.'

She held up a hand as if taking the oath in court. 'I promise, so help me God!'

'If you break your promise you break our love!' He was rather pleased with that.

'Promise on God's honour!'

He hugged her. 'That'll do me, Dolly.'

Dolly spent the night worrying about her mother's disapproval, but by the time dawn came she had come up with a plan to pacify her mother. She would find the vicar who had married them and collect the marriage lines. When her mother saw that she really was married, she would hopefully recover from her sulks and all would be well.

After breakfast she washed up the breakfast things and swept the crumbs from the table into her hand and tossed them into the sink.

Sidney had been very quiet throughout the meal, and now he gave her a strange look. 'That ring,' he said. 'Like to lend it to me for a bit? I'll take care of it.'

'Lend you my ring?' She stared at him in

horror. 'No, I wouldn't, Sidney.' He raised her hand so they could both see it. 'This is my wedding ring, and it—'

'It should be a plain gold band.'

'Well, it isn't, so there! It's better than a plain gold band, and I'm never going to take it off. Never!' She folded her arms and gave a defiant toss of her head. 'I promised on my honour, if you must know. Anyway, what d'you want with it?'

He glanced down at his fingers and then began to scratch at a greasy spot of butter on the crumpled tablecloth. 'Don't you want to know if it's real? I know this man who—'

'What d'you mean real? Course it's real. You're as bad as my ma!' She peered at it closely, almost squinting at the stone. 'It's a diamond. Satisfied.'

'But this man, Arnie...'

'Arnie? Who's Arnie?'

'A sort of friend. I could show it to him. See what he says.'

'What is he, a jeweller?'

'Sort of. You don't have to come with me. I could take it and then bring it back straight away. He might have conned you – Don, I mean. Might be glass. He might be making a fool out of you.'

'Conned me? His own wife? What a nasty mind you've got, Sidney. I thought better of you. Now drop it or I'll tell Don what you said.' She fiddled lovingly with the ring, then kissed it. 'You're a troublemaker, Sidney Wickham.'

'Or you're too gullible! Ever think of that?'

'What a dreadful way to talk about your own brother!'

He got up, staring at her as though about to say something else.

'What?' she challenged.

'Nothing. You've made your bed, now you'll have to lie on it! Don't say I didn't warn you.'

With hands on her hips, she watched him go, then stuck out her tongue at his retreating back. 'Make my own bed? What's he talking about?'

For a moment the exchange had distracted her, and she frowned, trying to recall her plan. Ah yes! She was going to collect her marriage lines – and to do that she must hunt down Reverend Willis Burke.

After a longer walk than she expected, Dolly found herself inside the Rose and Garter talking to the barman – a large man with a florid face who wore a dirty apron over a collarless shirt and moleskin trousers. There was a button missing from his braces.

The bar was empty except for one man,

but a small, elderly woman was wiping down the tables.

'Reverend Burke?' The barman grinned. 'The Very Reverend Burke?' He winked at the solitary man who was standing near Dolly, drinking his way through a tankard of porter and following the conversation with apparent interest.

Dolly looked at him hopefully. 'He married us a few days ago,' she told him proudly. 'I've come to collect my marriage lines.' The two men exchanged glances.

The barman said, 'Private, was it? One of those?'

'Yes, it was, actually. Simple, but nice. No music or anything because of the licence, but very ... discreet.' She smiled, pleased with her choice of word. 'Because we held the ceremony here I thought you might know where he lives.'

The porter man coughed loudly. 'Gone away, hasn't he, Bert? Our very own "Very Reverend"!'

'Gone away? Has he? Oh, I see! Yes. Most likely.' For some reason the barman found this funny.

'Do you know when he'll be back?'

Another exchange of glances. The barman said, 'I reckon he'll be gone some time.'

The drinker said, 'Gone to Timbuctoo.'

115

'Goodness!' Dolly smiled. 'Never mind. I've written him a note in case I missed him. I'll just give it to his landlady, and she can give it to him when he gets back. If you just give me his address...'

'His address? Ah!' The barman pursed his lips. 'Blowed if I can remember it. He moves around a bit.'

'Whenever his rent's overdue!'

They both burst into loud guffaws, and it finally dawned on Dolly that they were mocking her. Timbuctoo had been the clue, of course – she knew it was hundreds of miles away. Annoyed with herself for being taken in so easily, she took a step back and straightened her back. 'I don't think it's at all funny!' she snapped. 'But I can manage without you two.'

Robbed of their fun the two men fell abruptly silent and regarded her sheepishly, but she turned on her heel and walked out. To her surprise soft footsteps followed her, and she turned to see the cleaning lady, still holding her damp cloth.

'Never mind them, lovey,' she said, trying to see Dolly's face through dirty spectacles. 'Men are all the same. Their brains are in their trousers!' She patted Dolly's arm. 'Mr Burke lives at seventy-three Dart Street. Down there, turn left and left again.' She sniffed. 'Timbuctoo indeed.'

'Thank you, Mrs...?'

'Mrs Magg. I had a daughter like you. Pretty and bright. Nora. Lives in Ireland now with her hubby and five children. All boys. Can you believe that? All she wanted was one girl. But no. All boys. Course, he was a navvy. Nice enough chap in his way, but couldn't seem to give her a girl.' She looked at Dolly's swelling belly. 'Little one on the way?'

'Yes.'

'Well, let's hope it's a girl and won't grow up like those two oafs in there!'

There was a shout from inside the pub, and Mrs Magg rolled her eyes and scuttled back inside.

Slightly comforted, Dolly found her way to Dart Street and then to number seventy-three. Despite ringing the bell and banging with the knocker there was no reply. Frustrated, Dolly pushed the note under the front door.

'Please, *please* bring the marriage lines round,' she whispered to the absent Mr Burke before turning homeward.

As she walked home she found it hard to keep up her spirits. Sidney had been horrid to her, Don was away again on one of his trips, the two men had made fun of her and

117

she still had not collected her marriage lines. She had not expected disappointment to feature quite so early in her marriage.

George stood in the middle of the store and gazed around in surprise. It was more than a store, he thought. It was more like another world – crowds of people, counters groaning with enticing goods of all kinds, a murmur of constant chatter and movement on a grand scale. He had been standing there for a long time, or so it seemed, and he was unsure how he came to be where he was. Glancing around him he could not see his daughter, whose name he knew was Lydia, so maybe he had come here on his own. But why?

'Can I help you, sir?'

He turned to find a young woman in a smart uniform.

'I don't know,' he answered truthfully. 'Who are you?'

'I'm Miss Ebdon – a saleswoman on the cosmetics counter. I've been watching you and—'

'Watching me?' It was an alarming thought. 'I haven't done anything wrong, have I?'

'No, no! I'm not suggesting you have, but you seem to be waiting for someone and you've been here for nearly an hour.'

She smiled, and he saw that she was very

pretty in a modern sort of way.

She went on: 'I thought perhaps you were waiting in the wrong place.'

George thought about it. Was he waiting for someone? It was possible ... but if so he had forgotten who it was.

'I have a daughter,' he began. 'Lydia. And a son, Robert—'

'Perhaps we could find them for you. They are probably around somewhere. Were you planning to meet up?'

Dammit. She had interrupted his train of thought. '—Robert, who's dead, and Lydia, who...'

'Perhaps your daughter is looking for you right now.'

'I *think* he may be dead – or is that Adam? And we have a lodger. He's a sturdy sort of chap. A policeman ... Ronald ... No, Leonard.' Desperately, he studied the faces of the passing shoppers, hoping to see a familiar face. 'Can't remember his name, but he's a decent sort. Got his head screwed on the right way, as they say.' He nodded.

'Did you come here on your own, sir? You seem a bit confused.'

George gave her a sharp glance. She was beginning to annoy him with her stupid comments. If only she would keep quiet he might be able to remember. He noticed that

119

her expression had changed from polite enquiry to one of dismay as she began to understand the problem.

'Would you like to talk to one our managers?' she asked with false brightness. 'They could help you. I could take you to the manager and find your—'

'No!' For some reason the idea frightened him, and at that moment he became aware of a disconcerting rumble somewhere in the region of his stomach. 'I need to go to the lavatory!' he cried, and in a sudden panic he began to push through the crowd, arms flailing, elbows digging into flesh as he wove an erratic way through the startled shoppers who began to protest and complain.

'Lydia!' he shouted fearfully. 'Lydia! Where are you?'

An elderly lady, laden with shopping bags, wandered across his path, and with a rough swing of his arm he pushed her aside and hardly noticed that she tottered and fell. A young man with an armful of parcels then tripped over the fallen woman and also went down.

George shouted, 'Lydia!'

At that same moment someone grabbed his arm and shouted, 'I've got him!'

Some time later – was it hours or minutes? – he found himself sitting on a small leather armchair in what seemed to be a large office, and the young woman he had met earlier was trying to explain to a policeman that they were 'not prepared to charge him'.

'We're satisfied that it was an accident,' she insisted. 'The poor man is very confused, but we found out his address from something in his wallet and someone has been sent to collect him and take him home.'

The constable, young and eager for some 'action', glanced up dubiously from his notes. 'But how is the old woman who was knocked over? A Mrs Cope. And wasn't there a young man involved?'

George felt that things were getting out of hand. He did not recall knocking anybody over, but ... wasn't he on his way to the lavatory? 'The lavatory!' he said loudly. Yes, that was it.

The young woman beamed at him. 'You've been to the toilets,' she told him. 'Mr Robbins took you five minutes ago. There's nothing more to worry about. It was all a mistake. We understand that now. Your daughter Lydia will be here soon to take you home.'

The policeman, obviously satisfied, closed his notebook and put it away. He looked sternly at George. 'So you've had a bit of a fright, Mr Meecham. Took a ride on a bus and ended up here. You'd better not do that again. Caused a bit of a rumpus.'

George thought by his manner that he should show a little contrition, although he did not remember a bus ride. 'I'm sorry, Constable,' he said meekly.

The policeman tapped the stripes on the arm of his uniform and said, 'Sergeant Fisher!'

By the time Lydia and Adam reached her father she felt sick with anxiety. Her father's disappearance was what she had dreaded for months, and now it was playing out in reality and her husband was away on business. She would have to deal with the problem on her own, and she was shocked at how helpless she felt. Busy with a lamb casserole, she had assumed her father was still immersed in *The Times* as usual while Adam played with his toys on the floor beside him. Even when Adam had joined her in the kitchen to ask where he was, she had not immediately suspected the worst. Only after a search of the house, and a quick glance up and down the road, had she tumbled to the fact that he was missing. A further search in the adjacent streets and many frantic enquiries resulted in failure, and she and Adam had called in to the police station to ask if there was any news of him. While she was there a call had come in from the store, and they had taken a bus to the store to claim him.

'We've been looking everywhere for you,' she scolded as she rushed forward to hug her father. Turning to the sergeant, she asked, 'I heard that someone had been hurt.'

'No, ma'am. The lady concerned was saved by falling on to her various bulky parcels...'

The sales lady lowered her voice. 'And the young man swore rather unpleasantly, but it was only his pride that was hurt. Fortunately, neither is making a formal complaint.' She patted Adam on the head. 'Your grandpapa has had a little adventure, but now he is quite well, young man, so you and your mother can stop worrying and take him home.'

Quite well? If only that were true, Lydia thought despairingly as her father followed them into the taxi and settled on the back seat where she took his hand and kissed it.

'I'm so sorry, Liddy,' he murmured.

'You didn't mean any harm, Father, but you must stay off the buses in future or we might lose you altogether!'

'I will. I promise. I just don't recall ... That is, I have no idea how...' Frowning, he shook his head. 'It's all a blur.'

'We won't talk about it then, Father, but please don't frighten us like that again.'

Thoroughly abashed, George said he would do his best not to, and Lydia realized that in future she must watch him like the proverbial hawk.

Six

After supper that evening Leonard sat back and patted his stomach. 'That was a very nice casserole,' he told Lydia. He glanced at George, who was toying with his food and still showing signs of agitation.

Thus prompted George said, 'Very nice, Lydia. You may one day cook as well as your mother, God bless her!'

Lydia laughed. 'I'm not sure how to take that, Father!'

Leonard said, 'He meant it kindly, I'm sure.'

George nodded. He looked very tired, Lydia thought, and somewhat subdued. Probably the anxieties of the day had tested his strength. He had promised, without any arguments, to go to bed after his meal.

Adam was finishing his rice pudding, and as soon as his plate was empty, Lydia took him upstairs to prepare for bed. For once the boy did not complain or insist that he was not tired, and Lydia realized that the events of the day had exhausted them all. She read him a few nursery rhymes and settled him down.

'When can I have an adventure?' he asked sleepily.

'When you're a little older. Adventures can be a bit frightening sometimes.'

'When I'm five?'

'No. Maybe when you're seven or eight. We'll see.' She tucked the bedclothes around his neck and kissed him goodnight,

'Is Grandpapa going to run away again?'

'Run away? He didn't run away, Adam. Why should he do that? He loves it here with you and me. He made a mistake and wandered away and got lost and got on a bus and ended up in the big store.' Smiling at her son, she smoothed his hair. 'Go to sleep, Adam. I promise you there's nothing to worry about.'

'I wish Papa was at home.'

'So do I, Adam.'

'When will he come home?'

'Soon.'

'Only soon?'

'*Very* soon!' she said with a laugh. 'Would you like to say a little prayer for Grandpapa?'

Adam nodded eagerly and put his hands together and closed his eyes. 'Please God will you find Grandpapa when he gets lost because he doesn't mean it. And make Papa come home soon. Amen.' Opening his eyes, he looked at his mother hopefully.

'Just right!' she told him. 'Now we mustn't worry any more.' She settled him comfortably between the sheets and kissed him goodnight. When she left the bedroom she left the door ajar so that she would hear him if he called out.

'Very soon?' she whispered unhappily and wished, not for the first time, that John had a steady job and worked from nine until five. What would he say if she ever asked him to give up his work for the government? She made her way downstairs knowing full well that she would never be able to ask him, and that if she did, the answer would be 'no'.

George had already gone to bed. Lydia had given him a mug of Ovaltine and one of the tablets which helped him to sleep. He had fallen asleep within minutes, and she hoped he would sleep right round until the morning. To forestall any more discussion about the day's alarms, Lydia asked Mr Phipps about his day.

He considered the question seriously. 'Not a great deal going on round here except a fire in a stables at the end of Shardeloes Road. It's now a smoking mess, but the lads contained the fire very quickly so there was no damage to the adjacent properties. No one hurt, but the family cat got his fur singed!' He shrugged. 'Could have been a lot worse.'

'And the robbery – Glazers, wasn't it? Are you any nearer finding out who did it?'

He sat up a little straighter, she noticed.

'Well, things have moved on a bit, Mrs Daye. The man who was knocked unconscious has died, which means we're now investigating a murder as well as an armed robbery. We do have some vital clues – our witness has given us a description of one of the men who carried out the robbery, we're still assuming the driver is called William – and we do have a clearer idea of how the whole thing developed.'

Now he leaned forward eagerly, and Lydia could see how important it was to him. A truly dedicated officer, she thought, impressed.

'There were two assistants in the shop,' he went on. 'One of them female. There was one male customer when the two men barged in, passing the witness who was outside.'

'He was lucky not to be involved.'

'He *was* involved. The taller of the two men held a gun and threatened to shoot anyone who moved. While the second man smashed the glass of the counter display case, the customer took it into his head to tackle the gunman and, for his pains, he was hit on the head with the pistol and fell heavily to the floor. He lay there unconscious while the female assistant began screaming.'

'So no one was shot.'

'No, but the would-be hero is the unfortunate man who died of a head wound.'

'It must have been terrifying for the young woman assistant!'

'It was. She said afterwards that she kept screaming deliberately in the hope that someone would come to investigate. Quick thinking on her part.'

'I don't think I'd have been that smart! I would probably have fainted!'

'Of course you wouldn't, Mrs Daye. You underestimate yourself. It was all too much for her, though, poor woman. That evening she collapsed from the shock – although she later recovered – and took the following day off work. The second assistant wisely did nothing, but kept his hands in the air as ordered. Always better to obey in cases like that. No heroics. That's the perceived wisdom in the police force, although there are always people who feel the need to "have a go"!'

'I suppose they must feel responsible. If you're the manager of a jeweller's shop and the valuables are in your care, you may fear that you will be blamed by the shop's owner.'

'But it's all insured.' Leonard sighed. 'Gold watches, silver necklaces, a few diamond rings and a selection of valuable brooches, bracelets – the usual stuff which is easily disposed off illegally either in this country or in Europe. Probably all gone by now.' He shrugged. 'A sleight of hand! That's the way I see it. We sent out a list of stolen articles, but we're not hopeful.'

'And they got clean away?'

'Unfortunately. Escaped in a waiting car. And all we've got is a corpse who has now been identified. Married with young children.'

'Poor wife!'

'Indeed! A young family to bring up all on her own.'

'And a very lonely life.' Lydia reminded herself how lucky she was to have John even though he was away so much. Seeing that Mr Phipps now looked somewhat disconsolate she added, 'Your work must be extremely frustrating at times.'

He nodded, but then forced a smile. 'But we haven't given up yet. It's early days in a case like this, and now that there's a charge of murder likely the Met will put more resources at our disposal. We don't have much to go on, but we do have a couple of finger-prints.'

'Ah! I've heard of them.'

'Fingerprinting is a real breakthrough and will be more important as time goes on. There's been a department set up in New Scotland Yard, and it's going to revolutionize the system of detection.'

Amused by his earnest manner, Lydia smiled. 'You love your work,' she told him. 'I can see how much it means to you.'

He relaxed a little. 'It does, that's true, but my mother says I talk about it to the exclusion of everything else! Have I been boring you?'

'Certainly not. Your passion has impressed me, Mr Phipps.'

He rolled his eyes humorously. 'I've never been called passionate before!'

'Oh, but I think you are!' she insisted. Suddenly, without any warning, she found herself wondering whether he was passionate in his 'other life' – when he was not a police officer – and felt herself blushing. Perhaps her comment had sounded too personal. 'I didn't mean...'

Seeing her confusion he said, 'I know what you meant, Mrs Daye.'

Lydia struggled to change the subject. 'So am I now the best informed "civilian" in

London?' She chanced a quick look at his face.

'Probably.' He laughed. 'Mind you, we can't only rely on the fingerprinting. We do have our informants, and sooner or later someone will let slip something. The fact that there were three of them makes it more likely that there'll be a "falling out". No honour among thieves! And when we get them they'll go down – and the one responsible for the death will possibly hang! It's not called the full might of the law for nothing.'

Awed by his manner and obvious belief in the justice system, Lydia was inexplicably aware of a slight shiver down her spine. The full might of the law! The familiar phrase was being brought into sharp focus tonight in her own kitchen.

George had been in bed for nearly two hours, but although he was exhausted by his fright earlier in the day, he could not sleep. The unfortunate episode had brought home to him the serious state of his mind – something he had been trying to ignore for weeks. Ironically, the confusion he had felt throughout the situation had now vanished, leaving him with an unpleasantly clear memory of the disaster. There had been a pretty young woman called Miss Ebdon who sold cosmetics ... and an old woman called Cope – or was it Cape? And a young Mr Robbins had escorted him to the gentlemen's lavatories. What on earth had they thought of him, he wondered despairingly. A pathetic old man losing his mind!

Dr Wills had called in to see him and reassure Lydia, and that visit had further depressed him. Dr Wills was a familiar figure, but now, although he was not sixty, he was talking about giving up the practice because his wife's health was causing concern. A new doctor by the name of Lampitt or Norbit ... or was it Nesbit?

'Something like that,' he murmured. This Nesbit fellow would eventually take over. He would be what George thought of as 'an unknown quantity', and that was worrying him. In the past George had been able to talk to Dr Wills man to man, but a new doctor, young and with less experience, might prove less understanding of George's particular problems.

'Not good news!' he groaned aloud, but then stiffened as he caught the sound of footsteps along the landing and the flickering glimmer of a candle showed through the partly opened door. Possibly Lydia, coming to check up on him, he thought resentfully, to reassure herself that he had not made another dash for freedom. Closing his eyes, he pretended to be asleep as the door opened wider and she moved quietly towards the bed.

'Father?' she whispered. 'Are you awake? Do you need anything?'

Abruptly, he gave up the pretence. 'Yes!' he snapped. 'I do need something! A sharp blow on the head with a large hammer! Put me out of my misery!' He regretted the words as soon as they were uttered, but it was too late to retract them. Now she would be upset, he thought miserably. She was a tender plant and would take his careless words to heart.

'Father! Don't say such terrible things!' She leaned over him, and he could clearly see the concern on her face and was ashamed of himself.

'I'm sorry,' he told her. 'Forgive me, dear. I'm not myself right now.' Oh Lord. What a stupid thing to say, he thought, but he blundered on regardless. 'I don't know who I am, but...'

Lydia took hold of his hand. 'You're my father and I love you.'

'I'm a burden to you.' His voice wavered.

'Nonsense.'

'I know I am. I'm a burden to myself!'

'And if I were ill, would you call me a

"burden"?'

'Of course not, Lydia.' He sighed. He rarely won an argument with his daughter.

'Well, there you are, Father.' She smiled, squeezing his hand. 'I rest my case.'

Oh dear. She was being flippant. Trying to humour him. He swallowed hard, forbidding any tears to run down his cheeks.

'Mr Robbins,' he cried, apropos of nothing. 'He took me to the lavatory and waited outside the door as though I were a child! So humiliating.'

'Don't think about it, Father. It's all over and forgotten.'

He continued as though she had not spoken. 'And the old biddy I knocked over. She had so many parcels and a really stupid hat ... knitted with scraps of wool. All different colours. A small woman. Knee high to a grasshopper. That's how my mother would have described her.' He gave a shaky laugh. At least the tears had retreated.

Lydia asked, 'Did you take the sleeping pill the doctor gave you?'

He nodded. 'But it obviously didn't work.'

'Would you like another mug of Ovaltine and a biscuit? You may be hungry. You didn't eat much at supper.'

George felt tears pressing at his eyelids and blinked them back. 'That would be nice.

Thank you.' Anything to get his daughter out of the room, he thought bitterly. He couldn't stand her kindness a moment longer – it was undermining him.

Suddenly, he recalled being bullied at that awful boarding school. He had suffered the bullying in silence without giving way, but as soon as the house matron found out and sympathized with him, he broke down and wept ... Lord! How he had hated that school. His mother had promised him that if he wasn't happy there he could leave, but how could he have faced his father? 'Pull yourself together, boy!' he'd have said. 'I survived it, and so can you.'

Survival. That was all he had left to look forward to before he died. Now all he needed, he told himself, was time to think. There must surely be a way out of a future which was looking so dreadfully bleak.

Willis Burke's dreary room looked smaller than ever with three of them in it. Willis sat on the bed, which sagged alarmingly under his weight. Sidney stood by the window, keeping watch for any undesirables who might approach the house, and Don sat backwards on the single chair, his arms draped over the back of it. No one knew how to start the conversation which had now become inevitable.

At last Don said, 'So where is it?'

Willis pointed to the bottom drawer of his cheap wardrobe. 'Wrapped in a sack,' he added.

'I told you to hide it somewhere safe.' Don glared at him. 'Anyone could find it there!'

'You didn't say where. How do I know where to hide it? It's your stupid gun, not mine!'

'Christ, Burke, I trusted you to find somewhere better than the bottom of your ruddy wardrobe.'

'Like where?'

Don glanced round the room. 'Like up the chimney, maybe. Or ... inside a pillow. Use your imagination, can't you?'

Willis said, 'I tell you, it's not staying here. You take it when you go!'

Sidney gazed fixedly out of the window. His face was set in sulky lines, and he said nothing. Disaster was staring them in the face, he thought with a sick feeling of despair. This time it had gone too far, and he, Sidney, was not to blame.

After a brief hesitation, Willis walked to the wardrobe, pulled open the drawer and withdrew the bundle. He tossed it on to the bed. 'You look after it since you're so clever,' he told Don shakily. 'I don't want it any

137

more. You're the one that did it. You're the one that got us into this mess!'

Sidney said, 'He's right, Don! He was only the driver.'

'Only?' Willis scowled. 'If it wasn't for me you'd have got caught! If I wasn't outside waiting for you in the motor ... And all I get is a measly fifth of the take. Not that it was much this time. Less than half we got two years back. You two are slipping, if you want my opinion. A lot of effort and risk for not much dosh.'

Sidney said, 'Who are you to grumble, safely tucked away in the motor?'

Don chimed in, his resentment growing. 'Keep out of it, Sid. We're all in this together. We all shared the money. Remember that!'

Sidney snorted. 'But you got more than your fair share. *You* remember *that*!'

Willis said, 'What? More than his *fair* share? How?'

Sidney glanced at his brother and thought better of repeating the accusation. 'Forget it,' he mumbled.

'Nobody killed that man.' Don insisted. 'He fell and hit his head on the floor! I didn't shoot him.'

Willis jutted his chin. 'But why did he fall? Because you, Don, you stupid bugger, had whacked him on the head with the pistol!

138

They'll say it was the blow from the pistol that did for him. Likely it was, too!'

Stunned by the enormity of the disaster that had overtaken them, they all fell silent, each one a prey to fearful thoughts.

At last Willis said, 'You'd better scarper, Don. They'll be combing the streets for you. It's only a matter of time.'

'And if you get picked up it won't be long before we all get nabbed. Make yourself scarce, Don, before it's too late.'

Don frowned. 'Easy for you to say, but I've got responsibilities. You haven't.'

'What? The women? For God's sake, Don, how is it going to help them if you go down? They'll see you arrested, sent down and hanged! Strikes me they'd be better off not seeing all that. Do them a favour, for the love of God, and disappear. Disappear, and don't come back ... ever!'

The words sent a prickle of fear into Don's already burdened mind. Being a jewel thief was one thing – he had liked to think of himself as a daring, rather glamorous outlaw – but killing someone had never been on the cards. The death had shaken him more than he cared to admit. 'Thanks a lot! What a miserable pair you are. All you think about is yourselves. And to think I trusted you!' He glared at his brother. 'If it wasn't for me

139

you'd be working for your living and the reverend here would be finding out what it means to do a full day's work, scrimping and saving in a dead end job.' He rubbed his eyes wearily and sighed.

'I'm already in a dead end job,' Willis reminded him. 'I work all night for a pittance!'

Pale-faced, Don shook his head. 'And that's all you'd have if it wasn't for me.' His eyes narrowed. 'And don't forget that you're not squeaky clean either. A word from me and—'

Sidney pricked up his ears. 'Why, what's he done?'

'Impersonating a clergyman is a crime. Not to mention driving the getaway car. So before you decide to get rid of me, just remember that you two aren't exactly fireproof!'

There was an uneasy silence as each man considered these unwelcome truths. It was eventually broken by Sidney.

'So what do we do now?' he asked shakily.

Nobody had an answer.

Later that evening Willis Burke sat in his room with a blanket round his shoulders – not because he was cold but because he was frightened and had a sick feeling in the pit of his stomach. The wrapped up gun was on the bed beside him. His meeting with the Wickham brothers had done nothing to reassure him and had ended in Don slipping away with a muttered excuse and Sidney stalking out later in a thoroughly bad temper, having told Willis his suspicions about the rings which Don had held back and given, for the time being, to his women.

Now, nearly two hours later, Willis was still a state of utter dread, wondering what he should do to protect himself from any possible consequences. He could disappear by moving to another part of London, or he could stay and hope that the police never made the connection between Don and the victim, because Don had threatened to betray his two companions if he were ever arrested.

'He'll grass us up!' he muttered.

It also grieved him that he now knew that Don had certainly cheated him and Sidney by hanging on to a couple of diamond rings. 'Bastard!' he muttered. After all the things he'd done for that man! He shivered and pulled the blanket closer round his shoulders.

At that moment he heard the front door knocker and he froze. Was it the police? Desperately, he looked round for somewhere to hide. Beneath the bed was too obvious, but what about the wardrobe drawer? Could he fit in there? He rushed to the drawer and pulled it open, but then, remembering the gun, he paused and glanced back at the bed. 'Hell's bells!'

Footsteps sounded on the stairs.

'Mr Burke?' There was tap on his door.

He called, 'Just a minute!' and prepared to climb into the drawer before realizing two things – that he had given himself away by saying 'Just a minute', and that the drawer was too small. Also common sense told him that if he did climb into the drawer he would never be able to then push it shut and that anyway the whole wardrobe would probably topple over. Or was that three things? Or four? He uttered a small squeak of fright then closed the drawer. He must brazen it out.

Two minutes later, with a rapidly beating heart, he gave up, walked to the door and opened it about two inches. 'Yes?'

'A visitor for you, Mr Burke,' said the land-lady and to his intense relief he recognized the newly 'married' Dolly Wickham standing behind her.

Willis closed his eyes, uttered a prayer of thanks and smiled broadly. At that precise moment the devil incarnate, complete with horns and tail, would have been preferable to a police sergeant.

The landlady said, 'Another one of your sisters, Mr Burke?' and turned away, with a sly grin on her face.

Dolly came into the room. 'What's she sniggering about?' she asked. 'Does she think I'm your sister?'

'No, no! Er ... Take no notice, Mrs Wickham. The poor soul's a bit ... !' He tapped his forehead.

'How sad!'

'How can I help you?'

'I've come for my marriage lines, Reverend. Last time I came you were out.'

'Marriage lines?' Shocked, he somehow managed a light laugh. 'Dear Lord! I clean forgot, but I'll do it now. It's no problem. Do sit down.' He indicated the bed. *Marriage lines?* What on earth did they look like? 'So how are things going with you and Don?' He began to search for a notebook and, having found it, a pencil.

'Don't you have to fill in a form?' Dolly prompted. 'My ma's marriage lines is a form, and there are squares, and the man filled it in with ink. Name and address. Witness's signature. Things like that.'

'Ah!' He thought quickly. 'But this, my dear young lady, is a private affair, and we do things differently.' He found his penknife

143

and began to sharpen the pencil. 'And there need be no witnesses to a private ceremony.'

Dolly eyed the pencil with surprise. 'It'll have to be ink, surely,' she protested, 'because it'll have to last all my life and ... Well, it could be rubbed out if you do it in pencil. Not that Don would ever rub it out, but what I mean is...' She held out her hands in a gesture of helplessness. 'What I mean is, ink looks more proper, don't you think? More official.'

'You're right,' he said, deciding not to argue with her because that would inevitably lengthen the proceedings and he desperately needed to satisfy Dolly Wickham and get her out of the way before his landlady could ask any awkward questions. 'I'll do it in ink, Mrs Wickham. Anything to please a lady!'

'A lady? Me? Go on with you!' she protested, but she looked pleased by the compliment.

He hoped he had successfully distracted her. 'You'll have to forgive me today. I'm all at sixes and sevens. Family matters.'

'Oh dear! I am sorry. Not a death, I hope. I do hate funerals, especially if it rains. Even snow is better than rain. I'd rather be cold than wet, wouldn't you?'

'Er ... yes. I mean no – it's not a funeral.' He found a pen and an inkwell containing dried up ink which he resuscitated with a little water from the tap in the corner.

'Now please don't talk to me,' he warned. 'I don't want to make a mistake.'

'Then don't write me as Dolly,' she reminded him. 'It's really Jenny.'

He nodded.

Dolly pressed two fingers to her lips and that was when Sidney caught sight of her ring and was reminded of Sidney's suspicions. A question sprang to his lips, but before he could utter it Dolly gave him a smile of considerable sweetness.

'It's a shame, in a way, you being a reverend,' she told him, her eyes shining with sincerity. 'Never being able to have a wife or any children. You must find it lonely, and you seem like a very nice person.'

Forgetting the ring, Willis paused, staring at her. Was she teasing him? 'A very nice person?' he stammered. 'Oh! I don't know about that.'

'A very nice man,' she elaborated. 'Honest and true. My husband spoke very well of you. He recommended you, so to speak, when he wanted us to have a private wedding ... but I'm forgetting. I'm distracting you. Carry on, please.' She laughed. 'Ma always says I talk too much.'

'You could never do that!'

Dolly tossed her curls to acknowledge the compliment, and Willis found himself wishing that she had never set eyes on Don Wickham.

Reluctantly, he turned his attention to the notebook. First he wrote the date, then the two names. *Donald Wickham and Jenny Ellerway*. He underlined the names and considered what to say next. The pen nib was slightly crossed and not functioning very well so he must keep the 'document' as short as possible. While he deliberated, he sneaked a quick glance at Dolly.

A very nice person – honest and true. Willis was not used to compliments and he was surprised how good it felt.

In big capital letters he wrote HOLY MATRMONY then squeezed a capital I between the R and the M. It was looking good, he thought, but was it going to be long enough to look convincing? 'Date of birth for both you and your husband,' he asked, suddenly inspired.

Dolly told him and watched him write it down. 'Do you need our address?'

'Oh yes. Mustn't forget the address.'

'Number sixteen, Mansoor Street, Clerkenwell, London.' She waited, then went on: 'My mother disapproves of private weddings just because she wasn't invited, so I have to show her the marriage lines to prove it was all legal and above board.'

Ah! Her mother was going to scrutinize it. With an effort Willis tore his gaze from the delicious Dolly and concentrated all his efforts on the marriage lines which must be sufficiently convincing to satisfy a suspicious mother. He wrote:

I hereby declare the above persons justly wed in the eyes of the church and may the blessing of the Lord go with them to the end of their days. Amen.

Signed: Reverend Willis Burke

He added the date of the ceremony and read it out and was gratified to see Dolly's response. She clapped her hands in delight.

'That's quite wonderful!' she cried. 'I couldn't have put it better myself. Don will be pleased.'

He smiled suddenly as another idea came to him. 'One more thing,' he told her. Pulling open the drawer in his desk he produced a small stick of sealing wax and collected matches from his bedside candlestick. Carefully melting the wax, he allowed a few drops to fall on to the lower edge of the paper, then took off his ring and pressed it into the wax. The final effect almost took his breath away, and he wondered why it had never occurred to him before to use sealing wax. 'There you are.' He presented the paper with a flourish and a small bow.

Dolly studied it, her eyes shining, with obvious satisfaction. 'Thank you so much, Reverend. I'm looking forward to seeing my ma's face when I show it to her.' She peered closely at the seal. 'Are those initials?'

He nodded. 'My signet ring.' Then, without stopping to think, he said, 'Do please call me Willis ... if you'd care to, that is.'

The words echoed in his head, and he instantly regretted them. Would a real vicar ever say such a thing? It seemed unlikely.

It had obviously not occurred to Dolly. 'I do care,' she replied eagerly. 'And you must call me Dolly.'

She read the document aloud, relishing the words he had put together for her. For her and Don, he reminded himself guiltily. This sweet woman had thrown herself away on a man who, if he knew what was good for him, would soon move on and leave her and the coming baby on their own. She would be shocked and troubled by his summary disappearance, wondering why he had abandoned her and what she had done to deserve such treatment.

As if somehow prompted by his thoughts, Dolly laughed and wrapped both hands

148

round her swelling belly. 'I wonder if the baby could hear those words I read out? I hope so because then he'd know we were married.'

'You think it's a boy then?'

'I don't mind, but Don wants a boy. Men always do, don't they?'

Willis felt a strong urge to warn her to be on her guard, but that was out of the question. He wanted to tell her that the father of her child was a not-so-clever thief who had accidentally killed an innocent man, but she looked so happy, with no inkling of what was in store for her. She would soon be an abandoned wife with a child born out of wedlock and a 'husband' who was a wanted criminal.

He said hoarsely, 'You'd best get along, Mrs Wick ... I mean Dolly.'

'Yes, I must leave you in peace.' She began to fold the precious paper.

'Best to roll it,' he suggested. 'So the seal doesn't get damaged.'

She did as he told her, then carefully tucked it into her bag. 'I must be off,' she said. 'Oh! Do I owe you anything, Rever ... I mean Willis?'

'No. Normally, but not for you!' He gave a little bow.

Impulsively, she stepped forward and kissed the side of his face. 'Thank you again.'

A minute later Willis was alone again, with no wife and no child on the way. And no good prospects, he reminded himself with a sigh. It was a bad moment.

Seven

After supper that evening, Leonard offered to take George for a short walk 'to settle his dinner', as he put it, and Lydia watched them go with a feeling of relief. Since her father's recent episode in the department store, she had been afraid to allow him out of her sight, and the prospect of half an hour on her own was one to be accepted gratefully.

But she was not alone for long. She heard a key turn in the lock and was delighted to realize that her husband had come home.

'John!' She threw herself into his arms with a sigh of relief, burying her face in the cloth of his jacket.

'Darling Lydia,' he said, hurriedly extricating himself from her embrace, 'I saw them leave – your father and the lodger. This is a bit of luck. We have to talk about something, and I was wondering how to get you on your own when I saw your father and Phipps go out. They didn't notice me, thank the Lord!'

'They've gone for a walk.' She held him at

151

arm's-length, her face alight with pleasure. 'Oh John, I can't tell you how pleased I am that you're back. I have so much to tell you – about the other day when Father got lost and—'

'Not now, dear!' Gently, he disengaged himself.

'But dearest, I was terrified. He was gone for hours and...'

As she led the way into the kitchen she was still chattering excitedly until John snapped at her. 'I said, "Not now!"' He sat down then immediately stood up again and began pacing restlessly. 'We have to talk, Lydia, and we can't if you keep prattling on about your father! I don't have much time.'

'Talk about what?' Seeing his expression more clearly she was finally alarmed. 'You don't have much time? But ... what's happened, John? Are you ill? You look thinner than I remember.'

She reached for the kettle to offer tea, but he stopped her. 'Forget the teapot for once in your life!' Seeing her stricken face he took a deep breath. 'Sorry. Listen, Lydia, this is just a quick visit. I can't stop long, and I can't explain why but—'

'You said we have to talk about something? What is it?'

'Yes. Don't look so anxious, dear. I'm not

ill, but I have a proposition to put to you. Sit down, for heaven's sake, and listen.'

Lydia sat down, her nerves jangling with anxiety.

'My superiors are offering me a better job with more money ... a promotion, but we have to move from here. I shall be based somewhere in Scotland or maybe Wales, but it means we must move house. I shall have to go on ahead in a day or two and get settled in, and then I'll send for you and Adam—'

'And Father!'

'Yes, all right. George, too. It's all very hush-hush, as it always is, but you must wait here patiently and...' He swallowed hard, then brushed a hand across his eyes. 'We'll all be together again before you know it.'

'Oh, John!' She regarded him anxiously. 'I'm pleased for you for the promotion, but I don't know how Father will react to being in a strange place.'

'He'll have to get used to it! And Lydia, there's one other thing. I forgot to get your ring insured, so if you could please let me have it. Now. I'll see to it and send it back before I leave. On second thoughts, none of your jewellery is insured. I don't know how I could have overlooked it. Can you fetch the pearls and the gold bracelet ... and the little silver locket.'

Without another word, Lydia eased the diamond ring from her finger and watched him wrap it in a handkerchief and tuck it into the inside pocket of his jacket. As she hurried up to the bedroom for the rest of her jewellery, her mind was distracted by the prospect of moving from Lewisham. The very nice private school where she hoped Adam would be able to attend was now out of the question, but no doubt there would be somewhere suitable in Scotland or Wales.

'But why so far?' she asked him on her return, handing over the pieces for insurance.

'Don't cross-question me!' he said sharply, slipping the items into various pockets. 'I have to go where the job sends me. It may *not* be that far. I can't say yet.' Seeing that her lips trembled, he added. 'It might be somewhere nearer, like Kent or Sussex or maybe Dorset – but it definitely won't be London.'

'It was just that there's a very nice school where I hoped Adam...' She stopped as his frown deepened. 'I just thought...'

'Well, don't! I've enough on my mind without you whining about schools.'

Whining? Hurt, Lydia regarded him unhappily. 'But won't moving mean we'll have to sell this house? Father won't take kindly to that. It's his house, remember.'

'You never let me forget! He'll have to put up with it. If he wants to stay in this house we'll have to leave him behind!' Suddenly, he hurried into the front room, and Lydia followed him. He at once went to the window overlooking the street. Easing the curtain slightly, he glanced from left to right.

She stared. 'What are you looking for?' she asked, her unease deepening. 'Is someone following you?'

'Of course not.'

'Are you expecting someone?'

'No!' Cursing inwardly at her perception, he went on quickly. 'Look, Lydia, I know this has been a shock – a bit too sudden maybe – but I have no option. I need to move out of London soon.'

'Need to?' Her eyes widened. 'Does that mean you're in danger?' Instinctively, she pressed a hand to her heart. 'You are, aren't you? Oh God! You're in danger!'

He rolled his eyes. 'Don't be so dramatic, Lydia. You always overreact. It simply means I have to go where they send me. My superiors decide. You've always understood that. We just have to accept it in my line of work.' He drew a long breath. 'I'll be off now, but I'll write to you and let you know how things are going.'

'But John ... Can't you even stay the night? When will I see you again?'

'A few weeks, maybe. Just be patient, Lydia. I'll be working. I may even be abroad. If you don't hear from me there is no need to fly into a panic. In fact, please don't. You will attract attention to yourself, and who knows where that will lead. No one else needs to know of my plans, so for heaven's sake don't blab about what I have told you. Later you can explain everything, but not now.'

The more he said, the greater her anxiety, but Lydia simply nodded. Then she said, 'Don't you want to see Father before you go?'

'No.' He stared round the room, then took down the key and began to wind the clock. 'You can explain it all to your father in your own time. I'll go up to see Adam, but I won't wake him.' He returned the key to its place inside the vase. 'Wind it once a week,' he reminded her, 'and no more. It's a delicate mechanism.'

It had a terrible ring of finality, Lydia thought. As if John would never again be able to wind it himself. She rested her hand on the mantelpiece to steady herself. Stop this, she told herself. You are being ridiculous. You are becoming hysterical.

'Trust me, Lydia.' John smiled. 'This really

is for the best. I'll send Adam a toy as soon as I can. But remember what I said. Do not panic. And do not bring Leonard Phipps into this.'

Stricken with a nameless fear, Lydia sought for a way to delay his departure even for a few minutes. 'Oh, but John, I haven't told you about Father wandering off. The store had to send for a policeman, and for a while I thought...'

He held up his hand. 'Don't write to me, dear. Understand?'

'But John...'

He caught hold of her arm. 'No more letters to that previous address! As soon as I have the new address I'll be in touch.' He took another glance up and down the street. 'Now I must go.' He pulled her close and kissed her with a passion that surprised and alarmed her.

When he released her, she said shakily, 'What aren't you telling me, John? There's something more. I can tell. Please...'

He gave her a long, enigmatic look, opened his mouth to speak, but apparently changed his mind. 'Goodbye, dearest.' He moved into the passage towards the front door, and she ran after him.

'But you haven't been up to see Adam!'

He hesitated. 'I can't, Lydia. I just can't.

Give him a big kiss from me. Tell him Papa loves him and always will.' He swallowed and added huskily, 'Tell him to be a good boy always.'

Startled by his tone, Lydia put out a hand to catch at his arm, but he pulled away, opened the front door and walked swiftly off without looking back.

'John! *John!*' she cried. 'Dearest, wait!'

She was strongly tempted to run after him, to clutch at his arm and beg him not to go, but from behind her she heard a small voice and, turning, discovered Adam halfway down the stairs. His eyes were wide with alarm, and she wondered how much he had heard. With an effort she tried to compose herself.

'Adam, what are you doing down here?' With tears in her eyes she picked him up, hugged him and carried him back upstairs.

He didn't speak until she had tucked him back into his bed. Then he asked, 'Who was that, Mama?'

So he had not heard enough to recognize his father's voice. Thank heavens for small mercies, she thought. A white lie might be kindest. She had no desire to tell him that his father had been and gone without wanting to see him. She improvised hastily. 'It was a man looking for his cat,' she told him.

'Is his cat lost?'

'Yes, but he will soon find him, I'm sure.'

'I wish we could have a cat, Mama.'

'I know, dear, but then poor Papa will keep sneezing!' She managed a smile, but her thoughts were unhappy. How long would it be before they were reunited with John? The doubts crowded in.

As she tiptoed out of the room five minutes later, she heard her father returning with Leonard Phipps. Abruptly, she decided to say nothing about their forthcoming change of circumstances. What would she tell them, she wondered unhappily. It would all sound very strange. It *was* very strange. Lydia sighed. It was a very uncomfortable situation – frighteningly so, in fact. Perhaps she would be able to invent a plausible story that would raise no doubts or awkward questions. Slowly, she counted to ten and then took several deep breaths. She would wait until tomorrow, when she hoped her present panic would have subsided and she would feel more in control of her emotions.

Later that evening Lydia struggled against the urge to give in to her misery and weep, but the thought of her father's and Mr Phipps' concern, if they saw her with reddened eyes in the morning, stopped her.

Instead, she poured a small glass of sherry and drank it down in one gulp, promising herself that it would strengthen her resolve. Eventually, she would have to tell her father they were leaving Lewisham – and to tell Mr Phipps he would have to start looking for new lodgings.

But that could wait, she decided, until there was more definite news from John. Her father would find a move hopelessly confusing, and Mr Phipps would be disappointed at the prospect of finding other accommodation so soon. No need, she told herself, to make the situation worse than it already was.

'What a mess!' she exclaimed, fighting to settle her jangled nerves. 'What a truly awful mess!'

But it would be best, she thought, to let a few days pass until she herself had come to terms with the prospect, so that she could inform them in a calm and a collected way. There was no need for either of the men to know the extent of her own anxiety.

She found a pair of her father's socks and sat down in her usual chair, preparing to darn the heels, but before she had started Leonard Phipps had his own surprise for her.

'I've been thinking,' he said, 'about that strange letter you had about your husband's place of work. If you wish it, I could follow it up for you. My brother lives not too far from Mansoor Street. In Bidmoor Road, in fact. It's only a quarter of an hour's walk from there, and I'll be going over to see them tomorrow morning.' He smiled. 'They have a new baby – their first – and are keen to show it off to me. A little girl. Please God it will live.'

For a moment Lydia was taken aback, and her instinct was to tell him that it no longer mattered, but that would require an explanation. Better not to make waves, she thought. Better to accept his offer to enquire at the PSD office. 'That's very kind of you...' she began.

'I'll make a few enquiries for you at that address. I'll be discreet, naturally.'

Still Lydia hesitated. Was she doing the right thing? Now might be a good time to explain that before too long they were all going to find their lives drastically changed, but she did not feel ready yet to talk about John's recent hurried visit or the reason for his distracted manner. She heard herself say: 'That's very kind of you, Mr Phipps.'

'Truly, it would be no trouble, Mrs Daye.' He beamed, obviously pleased to feel that he was of service. 'It might set your mind at ease to know what lies behind the returned

161

letter.'

George had joined them and was settled in his chair and he began to show attention to the conversation. 'What's this about a letter, Lydia? Have I been told about it?'

'It's nothing really, Father. It's just that—'

'Mr Phipps seems to know about it,' he argued. 'I have been left in the dark.' He gave Lydia a sharp look. 'Strange letter? In what way is it strange?'

Leonard Phipps, seeing his mistake, said, 'Oh dear. Have I spoken out of turn? I'm so sorry.'

Lydia forced a cheerful smile. 'Of course not. I simply haven't had time to tell Father the details.' To him she said, 'My last letter to John was returned with a note to say that the firm was no longer located there. Mr Phipps happened to be here at the time I read it, that's all.'

'And where, may I ask, was I?'

Lydia was beginning to regret their lodger's kindly meant offer. 'You were in the garden with Adam,' she invented. 'I did mention it to you later, Father, at dinner. You must have forgotten.'

George said, 'No longer located there! Hah! Exactly what I've been telling you. What did I say, daughter dear? He's a spy! Always thought there was something odd about the man. He's a dyed-in-the-wool spy! Admit, why don't you?' He gave her and Mr Phipps a triumphant look.

Mr Phipps said, 'Really, Mr Meecham, I'm sure he is nothing of the sort.'

George glared at him. 'What would you know?'

'Father! There is no need to be rude to Mr Phipps. He is only trying to help.' Flustered, Lydia's voice had risen, and she cursed her momentary loss of control. She must not allow her father to see how much his accusations upset her.

George turned to their lodger. 'You see what I have to put up with? Bullied in my own house!' He tutted. 'My daughter treats me as if I am losing my mind; as if I were a difficult child!'

Embarrassed, Lydia remained silent, seeing no easy way out of the escalating ill-feeling. Poor Mr Phipps was now looking at her helplessly, and she could only roll her eyes.

George, however, was to come to their rescue. Leaning forward, he said, 'Well now, Mr Phipps. What about that walk you promised me – down to the paper shop, wasn't it – to settle our dinners? I'm ready if you are.' Pushing himself up from the chair, he looked round the room. 'Might take Adam with us.'

Lydia hid her dismay. 'Adam is in bed,

Father, and sound asleep.' She looked at Leonard Phipps.

Recovering himself, he said, 'I think the paper shop will be closed by now, but a quick walk round the block would do us good.'

George was already heading cheerfully for the passage, and Mr Phipps prepared to follow him out. To Lydia he whispered, 'Twenty minutes. It's easier than an explanation!'

'You're very kind, Mr Phipps.'

Keeping his voice low, he added, 'I'm sorry I spoke out of turn. I didn't realize...'

The front door clicked open, and George shouted, 'Come along, man! It's clouding over, and we don't want to catch a shower!'

From the front-room window, Lydia watched them go with a heavy heart as she considered the pressures upon her which were mounting day by day. 'Yes, Father,' she said aloud. 'It's certainly clouding over, and there'll be more than showers before long!'

That same evening, May Ellerway heard the front door open and expected to see her daughter Mavis returned from her work at the auction rooms where she was employed to dust the sale objects, sweep the floors and hand out catalogues. It was a job that required no training, little energy and very little educational success, and for these reasons it suited Mavis like a glove.

'Ma! It's me, Dolly!'

May turned from the kitchen sink where she was washing potatoes under the tap to rid them of the mud which clung to them. She watched her daughter come in through the kitchen door with mixed emotions. Soon the girl would present her with her first grandchild, but she had married a good-looking loser, in May's opinion, – if, indeed, they were legally married.

She dropped the potatoes into the sink and dried her hands. 'I suppose you want a cuppa and one of my tarts,' she said grudgingly, moving the kettle to a hotter part of the hob.

Dolly grinned. 'Love a cuppa,' she agreed. 'I've got something to show you. See! Read that!' She produced a sheet of paper and handed it over. 'My marriage lines. All present and correct, as they say. And it's even got a seal on it!'

May sat down, peering at the writing, impressed in spite of herself. She read it through twice and then, frowning, studied the signature. 'Can't read this name. Whose is it, the vicar's?'

Dolly nodded. 'The Reverend Willis Burke. He's retired from being a vicar, but he's still a reverend so he can do weddings

165

and write certificates. Honestly, Ma, I know you don't think much of Don, but you must admit he's done me proud – a private ceremony and handwritten marriage lines!' She beamed expectantly at her mother. 'Believe me, they're not ten-a-penny, but Don wanted the best for us.'

'Well ... What can I say, Doll? Maybe I was wrong.' To hide her feelings she busied herself with the tea-making, and Dolly found the cake tin and helped herself to a jam tart.

'So,' May asked. 'How are you in yourself? The baby, I mean?'

'Fair enough. It kicks a lot!' She laughed. 'Have you started knitting yet?'

'Mavis says there's not much point because we don't know whether it'll be a boy or a girl.'

'Or twins!'

May stared at her. 'Twins? You don't mean ... Who says it's going to be twins?'

'Nobody. Not exactly, but Don says one of his cousins had twins but one of them died. Twin girls. The first one born lived, but the second one died an hour later.'

'Oh, that's terrible, that is!' May sat down, her face troubled. 'So it runs in the family?'

'We–ell, not exactly. It runs in his cousin's family ... We'll, not exactly *runs*. I mean, it was only once.'

'Unless there was more that you don't know about. Like the cousin's mother or grandmother, maybe.'

'I suppose so. Maybe I should ask Don to find out for us. I wouldn't mind one of each. That'd be fine.'

They exchanged grins at this possible outcome.

'Twins! That'd be a turn-up.' May poured the tea and handed it over and helped herself to a tart.

'Bit different,' said Dolly, referring to the tarts. 'What jam is it?'

'Marmalade instead of jam. Mrs Next-Door gave me a jar last Christmas, and I forgot about it. You know what her jams are like.'

'Like glue!'

They both laughed. Mrs Next-Door, otherwise known as Old Ma Nortley, imagined herself as a cook, but her neighbours thought otherwise.

May said, 'I stirred a couple of spoonfuls of hot water into the marmalade before I filled the cases, to thin it down a bit. Seems to have done the trick.' Idly, she picked up the marriage lines and reread them, reluctantly admitting to herself that she was impressed – especially by the seal. Peering at it closely she saw that it bore an imprint of something, and closer inspection revealed two capital letters, slightly intertwined. 'Are these his initials? Looks like SM. Must have been one of those signet rings posh people wear.'

'Let me see.' Surprised, Dolly peered closely at the centre of the seal. 'It *is* SM ... but his name's Reverend Willis Burke.'

May shrugged. 'Funny ... Unless it was given to him by his father on his death bed.'

'Must be something like that.'

May said, 'Is his father dead then?'

'Lord knows, I don't, but if it was his father's ring, his father's name must have been Burke too. Perhaps it was his grandfather's. I'll ask Don. He might know.' Carefully, she rolled up the paper and immediately forgot about the seal.

May did the same. Through a mouthful of pastry crumbs she said, 'So, have you thought of any names yet for these famous twins?'

The next day Dolly went down to breakfast and found Sidney enjoying a bloater.

'I could smell that bloater right upstairs in the bedroom,' she informed him. 'It smelled so good it got me out of bed.' She glanced round. 'Where's mine?'

'Don't ask me. Ask your husband – if you can find him. He's supposed to provide for you now, not me.'

Dolly stared at him. 'You only bought one? You're a bit of a skinflint. All that family money you boast about and you only bought one bloater! You're a miser, Sidney Wickham!'

'I bought two, if you must know, but I've already eaten one.' He grinned.

'That makes you greedy as well as mean.' She stared out into the backyard, then said, 'Well, don't expect me to do your washing. Two can play at that game.'

Dolly's policy had always been to give as much as she got, but this morning her heart wasn't really in it. She had expected Don to be home by bedtime the previous day, and now it was nearly nine o'clock and he was still absent. She said, 'Does he always stay away this long? I mean, now that he's married...' Her voice trailed off disconsolately.

Sidney shrugged, then wiped the grease from his plate with a chunk of bread. 'Sometimes.' He gave her an odd look. 'You'll have to get used to him being away. Lucky you've got me!'

'Lucky?' She tossed her head and began to rummage in the pantry for something to eat.

'At least I'm a bit of company for you,' he went on, 'to fill in the long lonely hours!'

'I'd rather have a goldfish!' Dolly had just

169

abandoned all hope of finding anything interesting to eat and was spreading beef dripping on a thick slice of bread when someone rang the front doorbell.

Sidney sprang to his feet, startled. 'If it's anyone for me, I'm not here,' he told her, 'and don't ask them in!'

'Them?'

But Sidney was already letting himself out of the door which led into the backyard.

Dolly hurried to the front door to discover the identity of the caller and came face-to-face with a stocky young man who might, she thought, be in his mid twenties.

He held out a letter. 'I'm sorry to come unannounced. I'm Leonard Phipps. This letter from a Mrs Wickham came to my landlady, and she's a bit puzzled by it. This is number sixteen, so this should be the offices of the PSD, but someone has suggested that they are no longer to be found here.'

Wonderingly, Dolly took the letter and saw that she had written it. 'That was me,' she explained. 'I'm Dolly Wickham. I thought the poor woman should know that her husband now works somewhere else. There's no office here. There may have been one upstairs in the attic, but by the time I moved in here a few days ago, the firm had gone. All that's left is an empty room, lots of dust. Oh yes! And a small chest with no key.'

'So an office of some sort *was* here until recently.'

'Must have been, I suppose.'

'My landlady, a Mrs Daye, has sent letters to this address for some years without any problem. Her husband works for the PSD.'

Dolly frowned. 'Then why doesn't he tell her the new address?'

'She forgot to ask him because he was in such a hurry to be off again. He works for the government – rather secret work.'

'Secret?' Her eyes widened. 'For the government?' She stared at him. 'Is it dangerous?'

'I doubt it, but government business is frequently conducted without much of a fanfare!'

'On the q.t., you mean?' she said, tapping the side of her nose. She thought about it. 'But it *might* be dangerous. You hear things about people ... foreign agents and such.' She was warming to her theme, excited by the mystery and the possibility of skulduggery. 'There are lots of foreigners in London these days. Chinese and suchlike ... You hear all sorts of dreadful things. He might have come to some harm.'

'I really think not, Mrs Wickham, but thank you for your time.'

He smiled, and she wished that she could invite him in and make a pot of tea and talk some more, but Sidney was probably lurking around in the backyard and he'd told her *not* to do so. It was a pity because it all sounded very interesting. It would certainly be something to tell Mavis when they next met. To delay his departure she said, 'I'm married to one of two brothers, and we all live here together. Sorry I...'

'Do you think your brother-in-law might know something about the office? Where they've moved to, perhaps.'

'Sidney, you mean? Er, I'm afraid he's not here at the moment. Just popped out.' She felt she was rather good at lying – and of course he *had* just 'popped out', but only into the yard. 'My husband is away a lot. He's a salesman and travels all over the country getting orders. Shirts, ties, things like that. And not cheap stuff. High-quality clothing. He's away as well, as it happens.'

'Did either your husband or his brother work for the PSD at any time?'

'Not as far as I know. They've never said they did. I really can't help you.'

She watched him go with regret and went back into the house. Sidney had vanished – no doubt making an escape through the alley that ran along the back of the houses.

Returning to her bread and dripping she felt a moment's sympathy for the young man's landlady. Smiling, she finished her breakfast and thought smugly how lucky she was to have Don.

Later she went upstairs to the attic, to reassure herself that the information she had given the man was correct, and found, to her surprise, that the chest with no key had gone, too.

As Leonard turned towards his brother's house he was aware of a feeling of unease about his recent encounter. Mrs Wickham seemed pleasant enough, but either she knew very little about her husband and his brother or she knew more than she was saying.

He liked to pride himself on recognizing a lie when he heard one, but Mrs Wickham had been rather pretty and he'd allowed himself to be distracted by the bouncing curls and bright eyes.

'Shame on you, Leonard Phipps!' he murmured. 'A victim of your passionate nature!' Laughing, he passed a pet shop with a window full of sprawling puppies and a parrot in a cage, came to a small ironmongers offering regular deliveries of paraffin oil, and a barber's shop, then crossed the road and turned right again, still trying to quell his doubts.

Was it a coincidence that both brothers were out and unable to speak to him? And there was something odd about the firm PSD. What, realistically, could those letters stand for, he wondered as he turned the corner and strode on towards Bidmoor Road. The old man, George Meecham, obviously thought there was something fishy about John Daye, and he might be right ... and even Mrs Daye might have her suspicions although she was too loyal to share them. Leonard felt a strong urge to help her if he could, but would she thank him if he revealed an unpalatable truth about her husband?

On the other hand, if John Daye worked for a branch of MI5 he might prove to be a man of high integrity doing valuable work for his country and no one would thank a humble constable for interfering. He sighed. He would have to proceed carefully, he warned himself. A few words with the local postman might shed some light on the puzzle. And perhaps he would make a surprise call on the Wickham brothers on his way home.

That night around midnight, in a warehouse full of sacks of meal, bales of hay and bays full of grain, Willis Burke found it more difficult than usual to force himself from the safety of his shabby little nightwatchman's office and out into the warehouse itself for the first of his three 'security rounds'. Stuffing a ring of keys into the pocket of his shapeless overalls, he sniffed the dank air and took a deep breath to settle his nerves. Even with the miserable interior lights, the vast storage area was decidedly gloomy in the light of his torch and, to Willis's fearful eyes, vaguely eerie. Sinister even, he told himself as he stepped out into the silence of the area to be patrolled.

Tonight he was already discomfited by a meeting he had had earlier in the evening when a chap called Phipps had called unexpectedly at number sixteen while he, Willis, was there, watching Dolly and Sid eating pies and mash. Willis had called in to see what was going on and whether or not Don had made himself scarce, but the man was more interested in a letter and a man called John Daye.

'I knew that was a stupid idea right from the start!' Willis muttered, his words immediately lost in the vastness of the place. 'A bit too clever, our Donald!'

Phipps had been very persistent, and poor old Sid had needed to watch what he said because Dolly was there with her pretty little ears flapping. Willis had found the encounter very worrying, and the apparently innocent questions about PSD and the letter had smacked of an interrogation rather than a few general enquiries. Sid had thought so too. Too close for comfort. Much too close.

He was, in fact, hoping Don would disappear and stay disappeared, because if the police got hold of him they'd sweat the truth out of him and he and Sid would be next on the Wanted List! On the other hand, Willis was dreading a time when he and Sid would be thrown on to their own resources. Don had been the brains behind the robberies – the natural leader. That's what he called himself, and Willis wouldn't argue with that. Ever since they were lads he and Sid had followed Don's lead – and they had all done pretty well out of their life of crime. Without him they would be unlikely to carry on, since neither Sid nor Willis had any contacts. Don had insisted on keeping them to himself – for security reasons. That's how he'd put it.

'If you don't know anything, you can't let anything slip!' Willis spoke Don's words aloud. He'd been quite content not to be 'in the know', although he knew Sid resented the situation. But then Sid was a brother, and he, Willis, was only 'the wheels'.

Now, stopping to check some windows for signs of a possible break-in, Willis shivered as he tried to remember exactly how Sid had answered Phipps' questions. Had he, as Willis feared, given away any secrets? If so, there would be the devil to pay if Don ever found out.

'Does anyone by the name of John Daye come here?' the man had asked. 'Have you ever heard the name?'

No. That had been the safest answer, although Don had not always been a Wickham. He had been born Donald John Daye and remained so until his mother was widowed and was then remarried to a Thomas Wickham. She had changed her son's name so that the two boys grew up as brothers instead of half brothers.

Nothing wrong in that, Willis assured himself.

The problem throughout Phipps' visit had been Dolly. They had been hampered by Dolly's presence because if she had put two and two together the fat would have been in the fire. He had been aware of her sharp gaze as Sid stammered his replies.

'Has there ever been an office in this house?'

That was another one. He'd known that would come up. It was all Dolly's fault for interfering. Why had she opened the letter, and why on earth had she sent it back to the sender with a letter of her own? Stupid, *stupid* girl! In Sid's opinion, she deserved a good thumping for what she'd done, but then Sid thought women were like that. Always sticking their noses in where they didn't belong. The annoying thing was that they had not been able to tell her how stupid she'd been because then she'd have known everything!

And the way she'd looked at Phipps! She obviously had taken a fancy to the wretched man. Fluttering her eyelashes and talking in that coy way of hers. Good job Don wasn't around to—

He jumped violently at a sound from behind the mountain of sacks on his left – but it was only a rat. He hated the nasty animals, always slithering around in the dark corners, frightening the life out of him. They were dirty creatures. Someone had once told him that you could catch a disease from rats, although Willis could never remember *which* disease, but he knew it was quite disgusting.

He yelled at it, and it skittered away with a defiant squeak.

'Damned thing!'

He was supposed to put down rat poison once a week, but kept forgetting. He prom-

178

ised himself he would put down a double dose next time. If he had his way he'd burn the place down with all the rats inside it.

Reluctantly, he set off again past the place where the roof leaked. As he tried to dodge the drips, he returned to the question of Phipps. Poking his nose in where it wasn't wanted. Said he was asking on behalf of his landlady, who was the same woman who wrote the letter – which was Don's first wife, Lydia!

'We don't know what the initials PSD stand for,' Phipps insisted. He was like a dog worrying a bone.

'Well, neither do we.'

Willis grinned at the memory. Sid had him there. That put Phipps in his place, good and proper.

Regaining his composure a little, Willis moved forward purposefully, feeling a glimmer of satisfaction that they had managed to pass on almost no information to their inquisitive visitor. His own feeling was that the PS could stand for Public Something – that is, Security or Safety ... but since Don had invented the initials they did not really stand for anything. Don reckoned they were good enough to satisfy Lydia and that was good enough for him. The three friends had had a good laugh over the initials, which had been good enough for years, but now, of course, Dippy Dolly had to raise questions about it and they weren't laughing now!

'So what did you do with all the other letters addressed to PSD?' Phipps expression was almost challenging, Willis recalled nervously.

That was a tricky one, and Willis had felt quite faint at the time, but good old Sid had outsmarted the man.

'Burned them.' He had looked Phipps straight in the eye. The truth was that at this particular moment, Willis was full of admiration for Don's brother.

'You had no forwarding address then?'

'Nope.'

That had stopped him in his tracks.

Feeling happier, Willis started up the stairs to the next level where the main office was to be found. He always felt safer up here, nearer to the main windows so that if there was a moon there would be light from outside which made him feel less isolated. Glancing through the glass window into the office, he checked that the door was still locked and thought how easy it would be to steal something from here. Just smash the window, put his hand through the hole and turn the key. But then the office did not contain anything of value, so what would be the point?

'One more,' he muttered, minutes later, opening the door to the small stock room. There was even less to pinch in here. Old ledgers, printed sheets curling at the edges, envelopes, ink, pens, blotting paper, a mouldering box of business cards, a smell of damp paper mixed with neglect...

He helped himself to a business card, a couple of pen nibs and half a dozen paper clips. Not because he ever used them, but because they were the only 'perks' he could find and he felt he was entitled to something extra.

'Damn Phipps!' he grumbled as he left the stock room, locking it carefully after him. He had enough to worry about with Don about to leave town. How on earth would he and Sid survive without him?

Eight

When Leonard Phipps returned to his lodgings he found Lydia Daye alone, nursing a cup of hot milk. She looked so vulnerable that he almost wished he had no information to pass on to her, but she was bound to ask about the enquiries he had made on her behalf.

His brother always fed him well so he had refused Mrs Daye's suggestion earlier that she could keep his dinner hot over a saucepan of boiling water. After he had hung up his jacket he drew up a chair and took a deep breath.

Lydia flinched visibly.

'What is it?' he asked.

'I'm not sure. I have been anxious all day, and now I think you are going to give me bad news of some kind.' She shook her head. 'Poor Father has been particularly difficult. I had to lock the doors and hide the keys to stop him from going out in search of Robert. He was convinced that the boy had wan-

182

dered away and was lost.'

'I'm so sorry, Mrs Daye.'

She shrugged. 'It's over now, anyway, although I had to lie to finally convince him. I told him he had promised to call in tomorrow. I hated doing that because it just feeds his paranoia, but I had to do something. I'm gambling on the fact that by tomorrow he will have forgotten our conversation ... But tell me about your day – and anything you could glean about this mysterious letter from Mrs Wickham ... Anything good, that is!' she amended with a faint smile.

'Well, there certainly is no office at that address and maybe there never was one. There *was* a man called Sidney Wickham – odd-looking chap, eyes close together. He claimed to live there with his brother Don, and a Dolly Wickham was also present. She has recently married Don, who wasn't around, in what she described as a private wedding.'

'Private wedding?' She regarded him blankly. 'What does that mean, exactly?'

'I cannot say. I dare say I should have asked. She's expecting a child in a few months' time, and she was keen to show me a ring he had given her – a ring which looked suspiciously like a good quality diamond, although both Sidney and the other man called Burke insisted it was glass.'

'Burke?'

'Yes. Willis Burke. He seemed to be a friend, who'd just happened to call in. A rather nervous friend, I thought. He kept biting his nails and said very little, although he supported everything Sidney said. A little echo, you might say.'

'So, all in all, hardly reassuring.' She sighed heavily.

'No. It sounded vaguely credible, but in my job you get a feel for lies, and I'd put money on the fact that they were hiding something. They seemed frightened of saying the wrong thing – conveniently forgetting things like dates and names and insisting that they had never met or even heard of a John Daye.' He shook his head. 'The truth is I thought it all somewhat suspicious.'

'I'm inclined to agree, but I...' She turned as the sound of her son calling out alerted her to the fact that he had woken. 'Excuse me.'

After she had resettled Adam with half a glass of milk she returned to her chair, but had by then lost her train of thought.

Leonard leaned forward. 'Something particularly caught my attention. When I asked them what they had done with any other letters addressed to John Daye at the PSD

184

address, the brother said, 'Burned them all.'

'Burned them?' She was shocked. The seconds ticked past as she stared at him. 'How could they have burned them? John answered every one of them!'

'Exactly! And if they burned all letters addressed to John Daye, why were they adamant they'd never heard his name before?'

'Oh!' She covered her mouth with the fingers of her right hand. 'But that means ... What does it mean? If they didn't burn them they probably forwarded them to John? If so, then they must have a forwarding address for him.'

He sighed heavily. 'Not necessarily, but it certainly means that they lied. They most certainly had something to hide.'

'That could be true I suppose. What about Sidney's brother Don? Where was he?'

'Away on business. He's a salesman and travels a lot. The woman called Dolly told me that – before she was told to keep out of it!'

After another long silence Lydia said quietly, 'But whatever the truth is, no one has harmed John – as far as we know.' She stared down at her hands as she twisted them in her lap. 'Nobody could have harmed him because he still answers my letters and he comes home whenever he can. I saw him very recently.'

Leonard frowned. 'What put that idea into your head, Mrs Phipps – that someone has *harmed* your husband?'

Surprised, she turned to face him. 'I don't know. I think the idea has been creeping up on me.' She swallowed. 'I had a terrible dream the night before last – oh, you may think it trite to find a meaning in dreams, but...'

'Not at all. In fact I—'

'It was more a nightmare, in fact. I was walking in a very bad place, along a muddy path with deep rushing water all around me and dead trees in the landscape and a horrible silence everywhere and I knew it was a kind of Hell. Without the flames, I mean ... And then I heard his name – John's name – and there were grey sad-looking people all around me whispering his name over and over!' She shuddered. 'I woke up with my heart hammering, hardly able to breathe. It might have been an omen. I keep wondering what it meant.'

'An omen? I would hesitate to go that far, but I do think the mind can play tricks.' He shrugged. 'But you shouldn't let it frighten you, Mrs Daye.'

Her expression was bleak. 'But I *am* frightened, Mr Phipps. I have the feeling that something really bad is happening, but I cannot put my finger on it. I fear that worse is to come.'

After a sleepless night, Lydia came to the conclusion that she must somehow discover whatever was being hidden from her – but how to go about it? She felt intuitively that if she herself visited number sixteen she might learn more. At present the house in Mansoor Street loomed large in her imagination, associated with all sorts of nameless fears and unanswered questions. She now knew that there were people living there and one of them was a young woman by the name of Dolly Wickham. Lydia wanted to talk 'one woman to another'. Surely this Dolly person would understand her need for the truth. She decided to take Adam with her so that the other woman would be more sympathetic and hopefully be willing to help her.

As she supervised her son's dressing she pondered the problem of her father. If he went with them he might well cause problems, but after the incident at the department store she was reluctant to leave him at home unattended. She dismissed the idea of asking Leonard Phipps to watch him as totally unsuitable – her father was not his responsibility. She toyed with the idea of enlisting Richard Wright, who ran the paper shop, but decided against that. There was no way, she felt, that she could burden someone else. They would all go, she decided reluctantly.

Downstairs, she prepared porridge and toast for their breakfast and waited for her father to appear. When he did so she saw with dismay that he had buttoned his shirt wrongly so that the collar was lopsided, but when she tactfully offered to help him he refused the offer point blank so she let the matter slide. Really, she told herself, today she had more important things to worry about.

'I'm going for a long walk,' she told him. 'Would you like to come with us?'

As she expected, he agreed with enthusiasm, and by nine thirty the three of them had set off. Adam had his hoop, which he rolled along the unfamiliar pavements with obvious delight while Lydia did her best to keep a conversation going with her father. The journey took longer than she had anticipated, but at last, soon after ten thirty, they found themselves outside number sixteen. Even Leonard Phipps' description of the house had not prepared her for how ordinary it looked in the half-hearted sunshine.

She had become used to imagining it in a variety of ways, but number sixteen appeared as run-down as the neighbouring houses in the street, and she found it hard to visualize an important government office being housed there – unless that was the point of the exercise. A humble-looking place which would arouse no interest.

Her father said, 'Is this it? Is this what we've come to see?'

Adam, puzzled, clutched his hoop and waited for someone to explain.

Lydia said briskly, 'Papa used to work here, Adam, when he wasn't travelling.'

'When he wasn't out spying!' said George.

'Please, Father!'

They all stared at the very unremarkable house. The tiny front garden contained an area of dark pebbles set in concrete and two large pots, each containing a long-dead rose bush. The front step desperately needed whitening, thought Lydia, and the knocker would be improved by some polish. Before her courage deserted her she banged twice with the knocker and stepped back.

Adam said, 'Where's the park, Mama?'

'I didn't say there would be a park,' she told him. 'I said there might be one.'

'Can I roll my hoop?'

'Just wait a moment, dear.'

The door opened suddenly, and they were confronted by a young woman with blonde curls and a pretty face.

'What?' she demanded.

Lydia said, 'Mrs Donald Wickham?'

'Call me Dolly.' The woman waved her left hand to show off her ring and said, 'Who wants to know?'

When Lydia explained who she was, however, the young woman's manner changed. Brightening, she held open the door.

'Come on in!' she said. 'I'm the woman who sent back your letter. Want a cup of tea?' To Adam she said, 'Do you like kittens? I got him yesterday. He's a ginger tom. He's growing up fast. His name's Ginger.'

George said, 'How very original!'

Lydia glared at him. 'If we're not disturbing you,' she said as they followed Dolly in.

As they entered an untidy kitchen, George said, 'Good God!' and stared round in disbelief. Used to Lydia's tidy kitchen, he was astonished by the unwashed dishes in the sink and the debris of a breakfast on the table. However, he rallied, remembered his manners and said, 'I'm George Meecham. I'm the grandpapa.'

Startled, Dolly shook the proffered hand.

Adam had spotted the kitten. 'May I stroke

him?' he asked, leaning his hoop against the wall.

'Course you can, lovey. You can pick him up. He doesn't scratch.' She glanced round the room and said, 'Perhaps we'd better go into the other room. It's a bit of a squash in here, and his nibs will be down shortly.'

As she led them to the front room, George said, 'His nibs?'

'My brother-in-law, Sidney, the lazy wretch. Sit yourselves down.'

Pot calling the kettle black, thought Lydia as she sank into a sofa with sagging springs and a tired-looking cushion whose grimy cover needed a wash. There were dead coals in the fire grate and the room smelled musty. A bit of effort for half an hour, she thought, and she could have put the whole place to rights.

George remained standing by the window, staring out at the street, while Adam came in carrying the kitten with great care.

Dolly said, 'Don doesn't like kittens or cats because they make him sneeze, or so he says, and he said I couldn't have one, but he's had to go away for a few days so when he comes back I'll tell him I saw a couple of mice.' She grinned. 'A little white lie, but who cares!'

Without turning his head, George said, 'Where's he gone?'

Lydia was on the point of apologizing for the abrupt question when she realized that she did in fact want to know the answer.

Dolly shrugged. 'Lord knows. It's his job. Always disappearing. He sells things. He's a salesman.'

'Sounds like another spy!' George continued to study the street.

Dolly blinked. 'A *spy*?'

Feeling traitorous, Lydia whispered, 'He's getting very confused!' and tapped her forehead. Aloud, she said, 'I sympathize. My husband works for the government, and he's away a lot.' Searching for more common ground, she said, 'Mr Phipps is our lodger. He tells me you have recently married.'

Dolly patted her belly. 'He had to make an honest woman of me, didn't he! We had a lovely private wedding. It was wonderful. Really ... refined.' She smiled. 'Not a noisy crowd, but just the three of us. Me and Don and the Reverend Burke. He's a part-time vicar. Was going to be full-time, but I suppose he couldn't pass all the exams – I didn't like to ask – but he's such a nice man and we had this very simple ceremony and he gave me a little pot of violets which I'm pressing in a book and I've got this lovely certificate thing with a seal on it. I can show you if you like?' Breathless, she stopped, her eyes shining with pride.

Lydia was trying not to envy the young woman's evident happiness. 'That would be interesting. Thank you.'

While Dolly rooted around in a drawer of the sideboard, Lydia tried to remember if Burke was the name of the other man Leonard Phipps had seen. It sounded familiar, but she would check on it later.

'Here we are!'

Dolly handed over the paper, which did indeed have a seal on the bottom, and Lydia read it with considerable misgivings. Even to her unsophisticated eyes, there was something about the 'document' that lacked authenticity. Dolly took it back from her and showed it to George, who stared at it blankly, then shook his head.

Adam said, 'Ginger likes me. He does, Mama. And I like him.'

Lydia groaned inwardly. She knew what was coming next.

'May I have a kitten, Mama?'

'We have to ask Papa.'

'When will he come home?'

'I don't know for sure, Adam, but when he does...' Her voice faltered, and she saw that Dolly was watching her closely. She said, 'It can get lonely, even with a child and my father.'

A sudden sound from above made Dolly glance upward. 'Not much chance of being lonely in this house,' she said. 'Sidney's always hanging round. He doesn't need a proper job because he has private money, and it's so unfair because Don wasn't left anything! And then Willis Burke pops in from time to time. They're like three peas in a bloomin' pod!'

Unable to wait any longer, Lydia broached the reason for their visit. 'I wondered if you knew any more about the PSD that used to have an office here. I wrote to my husband here, and he always answered my letters so I know they were coming to the right place.'

Dolly pointed through the front window. 'Until a few days ago I lived over there with my mother and sister. Number fifteen. That's how I got friendly with Don, my husband – because we lived opposite. Also, we all went to the same school as young'uns – me and my sister Mavis, and the two Wickham boys. Not Willis Burke, though, because he lived further away and had to go to a different school because he was supposed to be clever and his ma and pa were a bit posh.' She tilted her nose up with a finger by way of demonstration.

George abandoned his study of the street and, turning, said, 'We were told by Mr

Phipps that you've never seen anyone called Daye.'

Lydia blinked in surprise, astonished that he had somehow retained that particular fact.

'That's right,' Dolly agreed, 'and upstairs there's only an empty attic which Don says was never a proper office. No proper desks or chairs or cupboards and such. And no staff – not even a secretary.'

Lydia leaned forward. 'Did letters come from other people for the PSD?'

'I don't know. Yours was the only one I've ever seen.'

Footsteps sounded on the stairs, and Lydia felt a dryness in her throat. A man called, 'Make us a cuppa, Dolly.'

Dolly raised her voice. 'Can't. We've got visitors come about the PSD. Make it yourself!' A tousled head appeared round the door, and she said, 'This here is Syd.'

'We told the other chap,' Sidney said angrily. 'We don't know anything about an office. Leave us alone, can't you!'

Lydia cried, 'But you know you burned the letters that came for Mr Daye. Or that's what you told Mr Phipps. But you couldn't have burned them because he answered them! So someone is lying.' She jumped to her feet. 'Anyway, if you burned them you broke the law. No one must interfere with the postal service.'

Bewildered once more, George looked from one to the other. 'Steady on, Lydia! What are you saying? Which letters are we talking about?'

'John's letters from me, sent to his place of work!' Her voice trembled.

Sidney said, 'For God's sake get rid of 'em, Dolly,' and withdrew from the fray leaving an uncomfortable silence behind him.

Lydia looked at Dolly. 'We're leaving, but don't think you've heard the last of us.'

Chastened, Dolly hesitated. To Lydia she said, 'If they are lying, I'm not part of it.'

'I know you're not.' Impulsively, Lydia stepped forward and gave Dolly a brief hug. 'I don't blame you,' she said in a low voice. 'You take care of yourself, and good luck when the baby arrives.'

Dolly brightened at the mention of her pregnancy. 'I could write to you if you like and say whether it's a girl or a boy.'

Oh dear! Lydia began to wish she had not encouraged her, but she forced a smile. 'That would be nice. If you give me a piece of paper I'll write down the address. I'll send you a card of congratulations.'

Dolly brightened at the prospect. 'I'll put it on the mantelpiece!'

A few moments later Adam, George and Lydia set off on the first mile of their journey home. George walked in a baffled silence. Adam, the hoop tucked under his arm, stared mournfully ahead, already missing Ginger. Lydia, her spirits lower than ever, was holding back tears of impotent rage.

A fitful moon cast shadows across the landing that night as George crept from his room. He was still in his pyjamas and slippers, and he made no sound as he reached Adam's room and gently turned the door handle. The boy lay fast asleep, soft muffled sounds coming from beneath the blanket which he had pulled over his head. George tiptoed towards him and eased back the blanket.

'Adam,' he whispered. '*Adam*! Wake up, lad.' He shook him gently until he awoke, rubbing his eyes sleepily and staring up at his grandpapa.

'Where's mama?' he asked suspiciously.

'She's sleeping. Don't fret, lad. I've got a surprise for you. We're going out on an adventure. Just you and me. How would you like that, eh?'

Cautiously, Adam raised himself to a sitting position. 'Just you and me? What about Mama?'

'It's going to be a surprise for your mother, Adam. She likes surprises, doesn't she? Now we've got to get you dressed and then we'll be off on the adventure. When you're dressed I'll tell you where we're going, so look lively, Adam.'

Adam glanced towards the window and frowned. 'It's dark! I want Mama to come with us.' He clung to the blanket as George tried to uncover him.

George hesitated. 'Look, Adam, the truth is we're going to the pet shop to buy you a kitten. If we tell your mother she—'

'A kitten!'

George nodded. 'A ginger kitten. A present from your Grandpapa! Now what do you say, eh? Are you coming or not?'

Slowly, Adam slid from the bed and trotted to the window. Outside, the street lamps flickered as slivers of thin fog drifted past making the familiar street look eerie and unwelcoming. He gave an involuntary shudder and turned nervously. 'But it's dark ... and the shop will be shut.'

'Dark?' George joined him at the window. 'Bless my soul, that's not dark, lad! The moon is shining and ... Adam!'

The boy ran past him, dived on to the bed and burrowed back into the security of the bedclothes.

Upset by this turn of events, George sat down on the nearest chair and wondered what had gone wrong with his plan. The boy wanted a kitten and his daughter refused to buy him one so he, George the grandpapa, would do the honours. What was wrong with that? he asked himself with growing irritation.

He said, 'So you don't want a kitten.'

Adam, holding the blanket up to his chin, peeped over the top at his grandpapa. 'I do ... but I want mama to come with us.'

George sighed. 'Well, if you don't want to share the adventure, I'll go on my own.' He stood up. 'One ginger kitten! Your wish is my command!' He swung up his right arm in a military-style salute and headed out of the room. He went down the stairs and out of the front door.

Shocked, Adam scrambled from his bed and ran along the landing to his mother's room and in at the open door.

'Mama! Mama! Wake up! Grandpapa has gone out in his pyjamas!'

She was wide awake in seconds. 'Oh Lord! I'll have to fetch him back. You stay here like a good boy and don't follow me.'

Pulling her coat on over her nightdress and pushing her feet into her shoes, she rushed from the room and down the stairs. At the front door she called back urgently. 'Go back to bed, Adam, *please*! I promise I won't be long.'

Rooted to the spot, Adam considered her words. He wanted to rush off with his mother into the darkness – *that* would be an adventure – but suppose he couldn't catch up with her and got lost...?

He climbed back into bed and reached for his teddy bear. The house seemed very large around him and very empty as the minutes passed and his fears deepened. Suppose neither of them came back...

But as she had promised, his mother returned with his grandpapa, and before long she had made Ovaltine for all of them and everything was all right again. Well, not quite, he thought regretfully as his eyes flickered and then closed. He had missed an exciting adventure and was still waiting for a kitten or a puppy ... or a rabbit...

The next day dawned with gusty squalls of rain. At number fifteen May was peeling potatoes when her daughter Dolly appeared at the back door that led straight into the kitchen. One look at her daughter set her nerves on edge because she knew that look – the pinched face, tight lips and furrowed brow. Even as young as six Dolly had signalled her displeasure with sulks, and May's heart sank.

'Now what?' she demanded without preamble. She pointed at the dresser with the potato peeler, and Dolly moved to the dresser, fetched the biscuit tin and helped herself to a custard cream. 'Honeymoon over, is it?' May asked her.

'Course not, but...' Dolly crunched into the biscuit, scattering crumbs. 'I just...' She sighed heavily. 'It's his stupid brother.'

'Doing what, exactly?'

'Meddling. Trying to make me believe that ... Trying to persuade me...'

'Spit it out, girl!'

Dolly took a deep breath. 'Making out Don's gone and left me. I mean, I know he hasn't, but...'

'Gone and left you? Gone where?'

'I don't know, do I!' Her frown deepened. 'I hate that brother of his. I really do. He's a miserable toad, is Sidney.'

May pretended to carry on peeling the potato, but her mind was racing. If what her daughter told her was true, Dolly's marriage would go down in history as the shortest ever! The Ellerway family would be a laughing stock. Desperately trying to keep her tone light she asked, 'So he says Don has left you. What gave him that idea?'

'Because he hasn't been home for a few days and...' She swallowed hard. 'He's working, I told Sid, but Sid shook his head. "He's scarpered," he said. He said this time he's gone for good and I won't see him again!'

Her voice shook, and May gave up on the potatoes and sat down opposite her daughter who was on the verge of tears.

'Don's never left you, Dolly, so don't be so daft. A lovely girl like you! He knows which side his bread's buttered, and don't you forget it. That bloody Sidney is pulling your leg. That's how big his brain is! He thinks it's funny. Probably jealous of his brother. That's about the size of it.' She smiled with false confidence. 'You mark my words, he'll be back! Don, I mean.'

'Do you think so?' Dolly looked unconvinced.

'I *know* so! I mean, what reason does he have for leaving you ... and for leaving his own home? Where's he going to go? Course he's not left you. He may not be the greatest catch in the world, but he's not a fool!'

Her words, May thought anxiously, did not seem to be having the desired effect. Please God there's no truth in it! That would put the cat among the pigeons and no mistake. She wouldn't put anything past Dolly's beloved Don, but they'd only been married a few days. It was a bit early for the fun to go out of a marriage, especially with Dolly's pretty ways and bouncing curls and the baby on the way and everything.

May leaned forward. 'Is there something you're not telling me?' she asked, 'because I can't help if I don't know what's going on.' Mentally, she crossed her fingers, praying she was wrong.

Dolly's mouth trembled. 'I'm not supposed to tell anyone,' she said.

May's hopes plummeted. 'I'm not anyone. I'm your mother!'

'Honestly, Ma, I can't say anything. I dare not because he might ... that is, *I* might make things worse!' Two large tears made their way down her pale face. 'Sidney made me swear!'

'I'll strangle that man!' cried May, her plump body shaking with emotion. 'With my own bare hands! I don't care if I swing for it!' She put a hand to her heart, which was thudding painfully. 'Just tell me, Dolly ... unless you want me to get it out of Sidney! I'll be across that road before you can say "knife"!'

'You won't tell Mave, will you? You know how she'll gloat! I'll tell her myself when I'm good and ready.'

'I won't say a word.'

Dolly took a deep breath. 'He says Don's done something awful and the police are probably on to him!'

May fell back in her chair, her eyes wide with horror, and for a moment she couldn't speak. She reached down, lifted up her apron and held it over her face.

Neither of them spoke for a long time, and then May said, 'Something awful? Like what?' When her daughter failed to answer she said, 'Dolly!' and slowly lowered the apron.

Dolly said, 'Like he's done a robbery!'

'A robbery?' May's voice was almost a shriek. 'What ... robbed a bank?'

'Not a bank. A jeweller's. That one in London. Him and Sidney – and another man who drove the car.'

'Godawmighty! If they catch him he'll go down for years!'

Dolly had closed her eyes.

May snatched the biscuit tin from her daughter and crammed a garibaldi into her own mouth. She selected two more and handed back the tin. Thus armed, she tried to think about what she had been told, but it was altogether too wide a picture. A robbery! Her daughter was married to a jewel thief! 'Too, too much,' she whispered. 'This is not happening. It *isn't*!'

'Sidney says he's going to scarper and that I should do the same because otherwise the police'll come after me but I don't know where to scarper *to* ... or where Don is and he ought to have taken me with him because I am his wife but Sidney doesn't know where he is and says he might be in France until things calm down a bit. But *where* in France?' Her lips trembled.

As May swallowed the last mouthful of the last garibaldi, her eyes widened. 'Where's that ring he gave you what was supposed to be a diamond?'

'Sidney's took it to a man he knows who'll tell me what it's worth so I can sell it and live off the money.' She tossed her head and gave her mother a challenging glance. 'It's my ring, and I can sell it if I like!'

May closed her eyes and groaned.

'Ma? What's the matter?'

'You've given the diamond ring to Sidney who is about to take off – and *he's got your ring*!' Her eyes snapped open. 'Yes! You may well look like that, *Mrs Wickham*! Trust me – you will never set eyes on either of them again. That's the end of that. "Finny", as they say in France.'

'Finny?'

'Never mind!'

Dolly glared at her mother in shocked dismay. 'Listen to you! I come over here for help and you make me feel a lot worse! What sort of mother *are* you?' She stood up. 'I'm going home, and I shall stay there. I still live there, and I don't need your help, so there! Stuff that in your pipe and smoke it!' She rushed to the door and along the passage.

'Dolly!' May screamed. 'Don't you dare run off. Come back here!' She raised her eyes heavenwards, both exasperated and infuriated in equal measure. 'Listen to me! There's no point in carrying on like this – you're in deep trouble, and you *do* need my help.'

Heaving herself from the chair she hurried after her daughter, but the front door slammed in her face and she at once gave up the chase. She would not give the neighbours the thrill of seeing her pursuing her own daughter across the street. They'd know something was wrong before too long. Word gets round. And how they would all laugh. One minute the Ellerways were celebrating a wedding, and the next it had all gone up in flames!

Leaning against the banister she drew a few shuddering breaths and muttered a few choice swear words before her anger suddenly evaporated, a sense of helplessness took its place and she sat down heavily on the bottom stair. Fighting back tears she rocked to and fro in an agony of helpless indecision and doubt. It was not long, however, before she gave way altogether and began to cry in earnest.

Nine

While May's day was being ruined by her daughter's alarming news, Lydia stood in the kitchen ironing and thinking about her visit to Mansoor Street and her meeting with Dolly Wickham. Her father and Adam were in the front room where George was helping him with a jigsaw puzzle so she was satisfied that they were both safe – for the time being.

As she slid the iron to and fro over her father's shirt she struggled to recall something that had been niggling at the back of her mind. Something Mrs Wickham had said had passed her by at the time, but had returned in the middle of the night only to vanish again as soon as she awoke. She eased the point of the iron along the left-hand sleeve and thought it had something to do with the kitten. So perhaps it was something Adam had said...

She turned the sleeve over and applied the iron. It would soon be too cool, and she would swap it with the other one which was heating on top of the stove.

'Ah!' She stopped ironing as the missing piece of her mind's jigsaw fell into place. Adam had told Dolly Wickham that he was not allowed to have any pets because animal's fur made his father sneeze! She smiled. Unfortunately, that was true. And Mrs Wickham had said that *her* husband was also affected by fur. She supposed it was rather like hay fever – the way some people were affected by flower pollen.

Finishing the shirt, she selected another from the basket and changed the irons. But Mrs Wickham had decided to get a kitten anyway, despite the embargo. Good for her. It would be a *fait accompli*, she reflected, and presumably Mrs Wickham was hoping that her husband would give in on the subject and let her keep the kitten. She wondered whether she could be brave enough to challenge John. Adam would be so thrilled to have a pet, and the animal would be company for him.

As her thoughts once more reverted to the newly-wed, she realized she had been quite impressed by the young woman, in an odd sort of way. Married for only a few days and already her husband was away on business. A coincidence, thought Lydia, because she herself had a husband who was rarely at home, so she could sympathize with Mrs Wickham – or Dolly, as she liked to be called. Not much fun though, she reflected, having that rather odious brother-in-law sharing a home with them. She frowned. Had John ever met the two Wickham brothers, she wondered. She found herself hoping that Dolly's husband was better looking than his brother. Surely an attractive young woman with Dolly's bright looks could have found herself a decent husband.

Now something else niggled at the back of her mind, but at that moment Adam came into the kitchen carefully holding the completed puzzle.

'Look, Mama! Grandpapa and I finished it. It's a mother cat and her kittens sitting in a basket. I did most of it, but Grandpapa helped me.'

His eyes shone with pride, and Lydia was again reminded of Dolly's stand. Before she could change her mind she said, 'I saw a little mouse last night, Adam. It was running about in the kitchen, and Papa doesn't like mice because they nibble the bread so I think we will have to buy you a kitten. What do you think of the idea?'

'Oh yes, Mama! I like it!' he cried.

Lydia quickly grabbed the puzzle tray, which was threatening to tip sideways in

Adam's small excited hands.

'May I tell Grandpapa,' he asked, 'or is it a secret?'

'You can tell him, Adam, and tomorrow we'll all go to the pet shop and see what they have for sale. It may be a black or tabby kitten. Would that matter?'

He thought about it. 'Could we still call it Ginger?'

'Of course we could! You can choose any name you like. Sooty or Tiger or ... Oh! There are lots of nice names.'

Adam ran off to tell his news, and Lydia followed him into the front room with the jigsaw tray, which she placed on the table. Listening to her son's excited voice and seeing her father's delighted smile, she whispered a silent thank you to Dolly Wickham. If only they did not live so far apart, she reflected, she might have invited her round to tea.

The next few days were uneventful except for the arrival of a tabby kitten, ten weeks old, which Adam had named Sooty. Lydia was anxiously awaiting a letter from John, but said nothing to anyone else about it. She was not very happy and became even less so when Leonard Phipps approached her while she was laying the table for the evening meal.

George and Adam were in the garden playing with the new kitten.

'I have a confession to make, Mrs Daye,' he
began.

'Oh no!' Dismayed by his manner, she
immediately expected something else to
worry about and eyed him almost fearfully.

'It's about those Wickham brothers. My
instincts tell me they are up to no good, but
I cannot put my finger on anything definite
so—'

'The Wickham brothers? But why tell me?'

'It was you who first alerted me to them. I
felt I should explain that I'm simply following up on my suspicions. All I have done is
pass on the details of my visits to them to my
superiors, emphasizing the mystery of the
missing PSD office – which you must agree
does sound very odd.' He looked at her
hopefully.

'What did they think?'

'That it did sound suspicious. They are
going to investigate – not mentioning any of
us, of course.'

'On what excuse?' Lydia felt distinctly
uneasy and annoyed that he had done this
without warning her. 'They might guess
and blame me!' They might retaliate, she
thought, but dared not put the idea into
words. The affair might somehow rebound

on John, which in turn might have repercussions in the government department where he was employed.

He said soothingly, 'They will pretend they are investigating something else – looking for a missing person, possibly. Your name will not be disclosed nor that of your husband. Believe me, you have nothing to worry about. I'm beginning to wish I had left you in the dark, Mrs Daye.'

Lydia swallowed, her throat dry. Had Mr Phipps unintentionally put her husband at risk? 'I rather wish you had, Mr Phipps,' she confessed shakily. 'Is it too late to ask them not to ... not to go ahead with their investigation?'

He hesitated. 'But suppose something underhand or illegal is happening. Isn't it better that we root it out? That way your husband can come to no harm.'

Slowly, Lydia resumed her task, setting out the cutlery. She fetched the cruet from the sideboard and placed it on the table with exaggerated care, trying to curb her growing agitation. 'My husband's work is very secret and sometimes dangerous,' she explained. 'I pray this does not affect him in any way.'

'I am certain it won't,' he insisted. 'Would you like me to keep you informed?'

She narrowed her eyes suddenly. 'Is this

going to upset Mrs Wickham? Oh, I do hope not! Poor soul. I'm sure she has done nothing wrong, and she's expecting a baby!'

Mr Phipps forced a smile. 'Might I suggest we wait and see what happens? I may have been mistaken, and if that is so we will be worrying ourselves for nothing.'

'You're right,' she agreed. 'I'll try to forget all about it. I know you did it for the best, and I may be overreacting, but I haven't heard from my husband for a while and that always makes me nervous. I shall feel better when the postman brings a letter.' She forced a smile. 'Worrying is what women do, Mr Phipps. We worry about our loved ones and the world in general! When you have a wife you will understand us better!'

Early next morning Mavis was outside the house, languidly sliding a supposedly clean cloth over the windows in an attempt to clean them. Her expression was sulky, as she had stayed home from work with stomach cramps and had hoped to be treated with a little more consideration. But her mother, leaving for the market, had said, 'If you're going to be under me feet all day you can do something useful.'

She was about to go inside again when she noticed a police constable heading along the street, and she lingered on the doorstep in the hopes of seeing something exciting. To her surprise he referred to a notebook he was carrying and stopped outside number sixteen. He knocked, waited, then knocked again, but no one answered. Mavis frowned. Was Dolly still asleep at gone nine o'clock, she wondered. Feeling rather dramatic, she hurried across and said, 'Good morning, constable. Are you—'

'It's Sergeant to you, miss. Sergeant Brandle – and what's it got to do with you why I'm here?'

'I'm her sister, that's what. Dolly is married to one of the Wickham brothers.'

'Ah! The sister-in-law.'

He seemed more interested, thought Mavis. 'We all call her Dolly, and I'm Mavis Ellerway. She may be sleeping late. She's expecting a baby and gets tired easily. I'll give her a shout.' Mavis crouched in front of the letterbox, lifted the flap and shouted, 'Dolly! Can you hear me? There's a constab ... I mean a police sergeant on your doorstep!'

The sergeant glanced up and down the road. 'I'm expecting a colleague,' he said by way of explanation. 'I think you should go back to your own house, miss. This doesn't concern you.'

'It does if it concerns my sister!' She felt the first stirrings of unease. 'What's it about then? She hasn't done anything.'

'Let's hope not.'

Another police officer appeared at the end of the road, and Mavis now began to suspect that all was not well. Sergeant Brandle began walking to meet his colleague and Mavis was about to renew her shout through the letter-box when the door opened and Dolly, still in her nightwear, whisked her inside and shut the door.

Dolly whispered, 'I saw them through the window. What do they want?'

'They didn't say! Maybe want to speak to one of the brothers.'

'They're not here. They...'

A loud rat-tat on the front door caused Dolly to back away towards the kitchen. 'Tell them I'm ill,' she said.

A loud rat-tat on the back door made them both jump, and then a face appeared at the kitchen window and a constable peered in.

'Open up, Mrs Wickham! We need to speak with you.'

'Gawdalmighty!' whispered Dolly, clutching her nightdress close to her throat.

'He's seen you,' Mavis said unnecessarily. 'Go up and put some clothes on. I'll take them into the front room.'

'Do we have to let them in?'

'It'll look suspicious if we don't. Go *on*!'

Five minutes later they all stood in the small front room: the two policemen looming large, the two young women feeling threatened.

The sergeant cleared his throat. 'We need to know the whereabouts of Mr Donald Wickham and/or Mr Sidney Wickham. They are to accompany us down to the station for questioning. I should warn you two that hiding information from the police is an offence. So where are they?'

'Gone!' said Dolly. 'You won't find them here.' She turned to Mavis. 'Sidney said Don's left me! Gone abroad.'

Her mouth fell open. 'Left you? He never has!'

'I tell you he has. Sid ought to know – he's his brother. And I reckon Sidney's gone too.' She turned back to the police. 'You can search the place – they're not here. They've done a bunk, the pair of them, and it's nothing to do with me so—'

'Can you prove that, Mrs Wickham? Can you prove that they've both left home? Two of them disappearing at the same time? It's a bit of a coincidence, isn't it?'

'Course I can't *prove* it. How could I? But you can search all you like and wait here for as long as you like – they've skedaddled! And if they're not coming back then...' Her voice shook. 'Good riddance to the pair of them!'

Mavis, confused, said nothing. If her sister was lying, she was doing it very well. But if she *was* lying, maybe she should play along. She said, 'I hope he rots in hell! He was never good enough for you.'

The sergeant was eyeing her steadily with an expression that she could not read. He said, 'Have a good look round, Constable. Start upstairs. Anything suspicious, we'll take it along to the station.'

'Er ... How suspicious exactly, sir?'

'Like jewellery ... or a pistol!'

Mavis gasped. 'A pistol?' She looked at Dolly, who was very pale.

Sergeant Brandle watched the constable set off towards the stairs, then turned back to the women. To Dolly he said, 'So what do you know about the PSD?'

'Nothing. I haven't lived here long. I don't know. Since I've been here I've seen nothing, but some people came asking the same question and I couldn't tell them anything either.'

Thoroughly frightened, Mavis said again, 'A *pistol?*' and clumsily crossed herself.

'Seen any staff around? Secretary, maybe?'

Dolly shook her head.

'What about letters? Seen any letters addressed to PSD?'

'One. I sent it back to the sender.'

'Were there any others sent here? Last month? Last year?'

'Not as far as I know. I wasn't here then.'

'So where's your diamond ring?'

Dolly was startled. 'How d'you know about that? Who told you? It was my wedding ring.'

Mavis whispered, 'A *pistol*? Oh my Godfathers!' and sat down heavily.

'So where's the ring?' The sergeant had moved a step closer to Dolly, and she tried to back away, but he snatched at her left hand where a wedding ring should have been.

She explained that Sidney had offered to get it valued for her, but then he had not returned. 'Neither of them are here,' she said bitterly, 'and I'm stuck here on my own with a baby on the way!'

Mavis, recovering slightly from her fright and feeling the need to say something helpful, tried to rally her senses. 'It's true though, Sergeant. It *was* her wedding ring. She *is* married. They had a private wedding.' She turned to her sister. 'Reverend Brook, wasn't it?'

'Burke not Brook.'

The constable was making copious notes

219

and did not answer. Defeated, Dolly and Mavis watched in silence as the constable returned from his search empty-handed.

'Nothing,' he reported.

Dolly said, 'I told you so!'

The sergeant said, 'Watch your tongue, young woman! If we find out you've lied you'll be in deep trouble!' He closed his notebook. 'And when the menfolk return – *if* they ever do – be sure to tell them we were here and we'll get them! And you two as well if you're implicated. I can assure you Holloway Prison is no picnic, so if you want to change your stories, best let us know right away.'

Saying nothing, the sisters stared at him dully, longing for them to be gone.

'We'll let ourselves out.'

After the front door closed behind them, Mavis and Dolly sat in silence for a few moments, staring at each other in shocked disbelief.

'Come over home,' Mavis said at last. 'Ma will be back soon. She'll know what to do.'

Neither of them believed it, but in desperation they both got up and headed back to their mother.

Leonard Phipps had gone up to bed around ten o'clock, but it was now nearly midnight and he had not slept at all – his mind busy with a number of matters. Some were to do with his job, and some were personal, but one was a mixture of both. When the church clock struck twelve he came to a sudden decision and sat up in bed. He would write the overdue letter to his mother, and that would mean that at least his lack of sleep had been put to good use.

Finding paper and pen, he began as usual:

Dear Mama, I hope this finds you as well as I am. Forgive me for the delay, but I have been very busy and had little free time to write.

I have settled in well with the Dayes, although the husband is hardly ever here and I wonder sometimes what he gets up to. He says he works for the government, but exactly what he does is a bit of a mystery. His wife is very kind and a good cook and looks after her four year old son and a somewhat con-fused father by the name of George. The truth is I feel sorry for her as she is obviously lonely...

He paused in some surprise and reread the last sentence. Was he sorry for her? He had not actually realized that fact. Was she lone-ly? She had never complained about her situation, but he supposed she must be. Was she unhappy? Having no experience of married life he had no way of telling. Thoughtfully, he went on with the letter.

Mr Daye is hardly ever at home, and I suspect she lives for his rare letters, which now seem to have stopped arriving altogether. Poor woman.

As for work, that is interesting and I think I have unearthed some kind of connection to that robbery at Glazers in Oxford Street. I did some investigation in my own time and then passed on the information to the nearest police station. I believe that two men who are arousing my suspicions may in fact be the thieves that are wanted in connection with the above robbery. Keep your fingers crossed for me, Mama. It may lead to a commendation!

Returning the pen to its place on the inkstand, he skimmed through the letter again and felt vaguely dissatisfied with it. Fearing that the letter read too much like one of his police reports, he searched for something more personal to say. His mother would want to share it with her sister and possibly with the neighbours. What should he add that would please her, he wondered. Ah yes!

The household now boasts a kitten, twelve weeks old and, house-trained. Although it is a tabby, little Adam has decided to call it Sooty. He is very thrilled with it, but I don't know what Mr Daye will say when he sees it as I'm told cat fur makes him sneeze a lot.

I'm glad to hear that your rheumatism is not so bad at the moment – that must be a great relief. Don't hesitate to buy more liniment or pills whenever you need to, Mama, because you know I will always foot the bill. It is no problem.

Don't worry about me. I am quite safe here 'in the smoke' and enjoying my new life. As soon as I can manage a few days' leave I will come home to see you and bring you a pair of London bloaters.

You are always in my prayers. Your loving son, Leonard.

He pushed aside the thought that his mother, alone now, must be even lonelier than Mrs Daye. Would she ever agree to leave Bedfordshire and join him in a flat in London? It seemed unlikely. It also seemed selfish even to think of asking her to consider it. Life was so full of problems, he thought wearily.

Sighing, Leonard found an envelope and

addressed it and set it aside for posting tomorrow. Which was actually today, he realized as the church clock struck one. Blowing out the candle he returned to his bed and fell asleep within minutes.

Ten

Mrs Duggett was happily ensconced in her favourite rocking chair, officially reading the latest copy of *The Ladies Journal* but actually dozing. A loud knocking on the front door brought her back to consciousness with a start and made her heart race. A glance at the clock gave no clues, and she heaved herself from the chair, grumbling, and checked her appearance in the mirror before moving along the passage to open the door.

'Mrs Duggett?'

She stared at the two policemen who stood on her doorstop with expressions which gave her no reassurance. To hide her dismay she said, 'Oh dear! What have I done now? Pinched the crown jewels?'

One, a constable, rolled his eyes, but the sergeant, a few inches taller, ignored the attempt at humour and said, 'Mr Willis Burke lives here. We've come to arrest him. Is he in?'

'Arrest him?' She had lowered her voice.

Having her lodger arrested would be a gift to her neighbours, who would gloat over her shame. 'You can't do that!' she protested. 'This is a respectable street. Mr Burke is a minister of the church. He's one of God's chosen. He also works nights, so I'd have to wake him up.'

'Get on with it then, because I have a warrant for his arrest.'

A curtain moved at a window across the street. It doesn't take long, she thought resentfully and wondered how many others were peeking from behind their curtains.

'Is he in or isn't he? You're his landlady, so you should know.'

'Maybe I should, but I don't. I was dozing. He may have slipped out.' She wondered if he could hear what was going on at the front door – and if so, was he making good his escape? Did he, for some reason, *need* to make an escape? It would be easy to climb out of his window and down on to the roof of the privy. Then he'd be out of the back gate and into the alley and away.

The constable whispered something to his colleague, who nodded and watched him run off along the street.

The sergeant's smile was cold. 'Alley at the back, is there?'

'Course there is. What's he supposed to

have done, my Mr Burke?'

'None of your business, madam. Now, are you going up to wake him or shall I do it? I can get a warrant to search the place.'

Mrs Duggett hesitated, thinking about the state of her home. There were a few cobwebs, shoes in the wrong place, laundry in the bath soaking ... She tossed her head, turned on her heel and went upstairs. What have you gone and done, Mr Burke? she asked silently. It would be a shame to lose him because he paid almost regularly and was no trouble. Not until now, anyway.

She knocked on his door. 'Are you in there, Mr Burke?' she asked loudly. Then, she lowered her voice and spoke through the keyhole: 'Only, there's two coppers at the door asking for you. Leastways, there was, but one's gone round the back to the alley. They won't say what it's about, and I've told them you might have gone out.'

The key was turned in the lock, the door opened and a very sooty hand grabbed her arm and pulled her inside. Her lodger was in his underwear, and she quickly averted her gaze from his scrawny frame. The door was relocked as Mrs Duggett stared round. There was soot in the fireplace and on the carpet. She tutted crossly and decided to try and make him buy her a new piece of carpet.

Surely, he hadn't tried to escape up the chimney. 'What's happening?' she asked, noticing for the first time how terrified he looked. As he scrambled into his clothes he was trembling, his eyes wide, his face white as chalk.

He pointed to a very sooty looking package which lay in the hearth, wrapped in newspaper. 'I have to hide that!' he hissed, reaching for his shirt. 'I was looking after it for a friend, but he's scarpered and ... it's a pistol!'

'*A pistol*!' Mrs Duggett took a step backwards, one hand on her heart.

'Shh! It's not loaded. You're quite safe. What do they want?'

'They've come to arrest you. That's what they said.'

Before either of them could decide what was best to be done, they heard heavy footsteps on the stairs.

A deep voice said, 'I'm coming up, Mr Burke, and I want no nonsense from you.'

'That's the sergeant.' Mrs Duggett wrapped her arms around herself defensively. 'You'd best go quietly, Mr Burke,' she suggested. 'You don't want it to end in fisticuffs. There are two of them, and if you try and fight back they might say you were trying to...'

When the footsteps reached the landing

they speeded up and the door was thrown open. The sergeant stepped into the room and glanced round, noting the rumpled bed. 'Willis Burke, I am Sergeant Harris, and I'm arresting you on a charge of—'

'I was never in the shop!' Burke stammered, sinking back on to the bed. 'I was just the driver!'

Ignoring him, the sergeant continued: '— of fraud and misleading the public and obtaining money by false pretences. Anything you say may be used in evidence against you.'

He stammered 'I – I don't know what you mean. Fraud? Wh–what's that about? Mrs Duggett will tell you I'm a model citizen. She'll vouch for me.' He looked at her imploringly.

Mrs Duggett, however, had gone as far as she was prepared to go to help him. 'Vouch, indeed! Don't you go dragging me into whatever it is. And what's that about a shop? I know nothing about any shop.' She turned back to the policeman. 'It's nothing to do with me. I don't know what he does with his time.'

The sergeant grinned. 'Hardly a character reference!' he sneered. 'We'll have to see what he says down at the station.' He grabbed his prisoner by the arm and yanked him to his feet.

Seeing her lodger's terrified expression, Mrs Duggett relented slightly and added, 'But I don't reckon he's done anything wrong, Sergeant, because he's a man of God.'

'Oh yes? Is that what he says?'

'It's true!'

'That's a matter of opinion.' He pushed his face close to Willis Burke's. 'Ever heard of a private wedding, Mr Burke?'

She went on as if he had not spoken. 'A man of the cloth, as they say. He wouldn't hurt a fly!'

'Oh, wouldn't he? I think Mrs May Ellerway would see it differently!' He frowned at the mess in the hearth. 'What's all this soot then? Made a right mess.'

Mrs Duggett rallied. 'A bird came down the chimney. A pigeon. They do that. They get stuck, then they panic and fly down instead of up.' She smiled at her lodger. 'Always gives you a bit of a fright, doesn't it, Mr Burke? Mind you–' she turned to the sergeant – 'I'm expecting him to pay for a new bit of carpet, 'cos I told him to stuff some newspaper up the chimney and he hasn't bothered. So this mess—'

'I will do it. Yes.' Her lodger nodded eagerly, but the policeman had lost interest in the soot. Very deliberately, he pulled handcuffs from his pocket. 'Please hold out your hands, Mr Burke.'

'But I'm not guilty! I haven't done anything!'

'I shan't ask again. Are you resisting arrest?'

'No, but I ... Well, not exactly.' Closing his eyes, Willis Burke held out his hands.

The sergeant snapped the handcuffs around his wrists. 'You are charged with falsifying marriage documents and impersonating a vicar!' He looked out of the window and signalled to his colleague, who had found his way to the back alley and was waiting at the back gate. Pushing up the lower sash window he shouted, 'Get back here pronto, Constable! We've got him.'

Minutes later, as a shocked Mrs Duggett watched, the three of them left and closed the door behind them. She was aware, in the ensuing silence, of a sense of loss, and was thoroughly unsettled, but by the time she had made a pot of tea, Maggie, her next-door neighbour, was knocking on the door demanding to know what was going on. Telling the exciting story of her lodger's arrest cheered Mrs Duggett up again.

Maggie said, 'Lodgers come and go, Mrs Duggett. You'll soon find someone else.'

It wasn't until the next morning, when Mrs Duggett went into Mr Burke's room to tidy up and strip the bed, that the landlady found the pistol under the pillow, and wondering what to do with it unsettled her again.

While Willis Burke was being arrested, Lydia was peeling potatoes for their evening meal and finally allowing herself to think the unthinkable about the man she loved. Her peeling knife moved slowly as the minutes passed and the peelings fell softly into the tin bowl in the sink. As her painful thoughts whirled, she added the finished potato to those already in the water in the saucepan and her hand reached automatically for another ... and then another, until her conclusions became an agony of despair and she uttered a faint cry that was almost a sob. She dropped the potato, the knife fell from her hand, and she staggered back, her hands groping blindly to find somewhere to sit before she fell. Seated, she stared vacantly, her face was pale and her breathing laboured.

'John!' she whispered. *'John!'*

He was never coming back! He had gone ... somewhere. He was obviously in danger from those unseen enemies of the country's government. The tell-tale signs were there, she told herself, but she had ignored them. John had taken her jewellery 'to get it insured' and would never return it because he needed money, because he was being pursued. If he returned to them, she and Adam and her Father would also be in danger.

'Oh John! My dearest!'

He had not been able to say goodbye to his son because he was forced by circumstances beyond his control to desert them – to protect them, most likely, she thought. Whatever threatened him meant that he'd had no option but to put his wife and child at a safe distance. But what was it that threatened him?

'Something is terribly wrong!' she murmured.

The vague doubts and worries that had afflicted her throughout the past weeks had suddenly crystallized into something that felt like a certainty.

She said, 'John!' and felt her stomach churn. Why did she feel so certain that she would never see him again? How did she *know* that he would never again hold her in his arms or wake beside her in their bed? Her body felt leaden, and she could scarcely see across the kitchen. She felt shocked and so cold. Was she going to faint? 'No, do not lose control!' she told herself.

She could hear Mr Phipps and Adam in the backyard. The latter was trying to teach the kitten to fetch a ball.

'He's not like a puppy,' Mr Phipps explained. 'He'll run after it, but he won't bring it back.'

'Why won't he?'

'Because he doesn't understand what you want him to do. He just wants to play with it. Cats don't learn tricks the way dogs do.'

'But why don't they?'

'Nobody knows, Adam, but they don't.'

Lydia closed her eyes. 'I'm going to be sick!' she whispered and stumbled towards the sink. Pulling out a bucket from beneath it, she threw up the contents of her stomach as tears forced themselves down her cheeks.

'My dear, Liddy! You're ill!'

Her father had come in from the front room and now hurried to her, his face creased with concern. 'My dear, you must go upstairs and rest. I'll bring you a cup of tea.'

Looking into his familiar face, Lydia was suddenly reminded of years past, before he had started to change, and that provoked more tears. A moment later she was on her feet and he was holding her in his arms, patting her back gently and murmuring soothing words which brought a small glow of comfort. Clinging to him, she smelled the familiar mix of his shaving soap and pipe tobacco – a smell which carried her back to her childhood when she would run into his arms on his return from the shop. Always he had a biscuit for her, hidden in his jacket pocket.

'I'll help you upstairs, Liddy, and then I'll put the kettle on and bring you some tea – or maybe some Ovaltine. You can rest. I'll see to the bucket. Now come along, dear.'

Gratefully, she allowed him to help her up the stairs, his arm around her waist. When they reached her bedroom he watched her climb on to the bed.

He said gently, 'Whatever has happened, Lydia, you are not alone. You still have me and little Adam.'

Astonished by his perception, Lydia blotted her tears on the sheet and closed her eyes. After he had gone she finally acknowledged that what she had always dreaded was happening. She was losing her husband, and Adam was losing his father. Their future was bleak.

When Leonard Phipps came back indoors with Adam and the kitten, Sooty fell into his basket and went to sleep. George took the lodger on one side and explained that Mrs Daye was unwell. He found a new puzzle for

Adam and settled him in the front room, before leading Mr Phipps back into the kitchen and sitting him down. Then he sat down beside him and leaned forward.

'I'm worried about my daughter,' he said without preamble, 'and I'd be glad if you would help keep an eye open for any signs of distress. The fact is that she has had a bad shock – she has come to the conclusion that all is not well with her husband and that he may have left her.'

'Left her? Good Lord!'

'I've had my suspicions from the day I met him. All this unnatural secrecy about where he is and what he is doing. I don't think he really works for the government, and I believe it has just dawned on her that ... Well.' He shrugged. 'That he is in some kind of trouble. I noticed she was no longer wearing her diamond ring, and she admits he has taken back all her jewellery. Presents he gave her over the years. Says he's getting them insured. That's poppycock!'

'But the PSD? Couldn't we—'

'There's no such place – in my opinion. Just a red herring. He's spun her a yarn, and she fell for it. Poor Lydia. Why she married him is a mystery to me.'

'I did find all that rather odd, I must admit, but it wasn't my place to—'

'Well, now it is!' George tapped the side of his nose. 'She thinks I'm in my dotage, and I may not be the man I was five years ago, but I'm not completely daft yet! Sometimes I get muddled, but most of the time I know which day it is and who's on the throne!' He gave a short laugh. 'Don't ask me. I might say Queen Victoria!'

'I wouldn't dream of—'

'I'm usually fairly lucid, so far so good, but my father went this way, poor old boy. It's not easy getting old, but you've a long way to go...' He took out his pocket watch, opened the back and blew gently into it. Closing it, he checked the time. 'Ah yes! This watch keeps pretty good time. Yes ... A nice little timepiece. I shall leave it to Robert when I die.' He slipped it back into his waistcoat pocket. 'Where was I, Mr Phipps?'

'We spoke about your daughter and her husband and where he is now.'

'Ah! So we did. Yes, I see what goes on, but I bide my time.'

Mr Phipps was looking very worried, thought George, as well he should. He was a policeman, and he was in a better position to discover the truth – if he cared to make the effort.

'So, Mr Meecham, you don't really think he is a spy – or do you?' Mr Phipps asked.

'No. Not sufficiently well educated to be a spy. They don't take just anybody, and that's what he is – just anybody. No, he's up to something, and he may well be in danger now, but I doubt the government knows anything about him.'

'I'll do whatever I can to help you.'

'Thank you. He's a wrong'un! That's all I know, and I don't want him ruining my daughter's life – if he hasn't already done so.' He glanced round. 'Where's the boy gone, I wonder? Where's young Robert?'

'*Adam* is in the other room doing his puzzle.'

'Adam? Oh yes, of course.' He rose slowly to his feet, suddenly feeling exhausted by his extended conversation. 'I promised Liddy a mug of Ovaltine, so she will be wondering where it is and thinking I've forgotten.' He put a finger to his lips and nodded towards upstairs where Lydia was resting. 'Not a word!'

'Of course not, sir.'

'I thought two heads would be better than one, and we *do* have a problem.'

'You can rely on me.'

George smiled. 'I thought that would be your answer.' He stared round the room in search of inspiration. 'Now, where was I going?'

★ ★ ★

The interview room was small and simply furnished with a table and two chairs, a coat stand, and a waste-paper basket made of raffia. Willis Burke viewed it with distaste. He regarded the sergeant sullenly and said, 'It stinks in here!'

'That's the smell of fear, Mr Burke.' The policeman laughed. 'No doubt you'll be adding to it in a minute. Sit down. You need to answer a few questions for us.'

'And then I can go?'

'Maybe, and then again maybe not.'

Burke removed his cap and folded it into a roll, then sat down after brushing some imaginary specks of dirt from the chair. He had decided to put on a show of bravado, but inside he was trembling and his mind was racing. What could he say and what must he conceal? He must watch out for trick questions. The police were very good at that.

'Name?'

'Willis Burke.'

'Not a reverend, then?'

His pulse speeded up, and his grip on his cap tightened. Was this really what it was about? 'I didn't pass the exams. I could have been a vicar. I studied it all ... Well, not quite all, but enough. I had to give up because ...

239

of ill health.'

'Ah yes. St Joseph's, wasn't it?'

'Who told you I'd been to college? Who told you I was at St Joseph's? I bet I know!'

'So do you have any real qualifications to do with the church?'

'I told you I couldn't take the examinations. I can guess who told *you* I didn't. That so-called friend! If I ever see him again...'

'And this friend? His name, please.'

'I'm not saying his name. You can't drag him into this.'

'Not even if he's dragged *you* into it?'

Burke hated the man's sly smile – the cat with a mouse. He remained silent. He would outwit this sergeant, he vowed.

'Mr Burke, are you or are you not qualified to take religious services?'

'Yes ... At least, in a private way. That is, sort of.' He studied the man, hating his moustache and his red face and his hands with their big fingers. Like sausages. Instinctively, he glanced at his own hands, preferring his slim fingers, which his aunt had once described as artistic – much to his mother's delight.

'So would you call a wedding a religious service, Mr Burke, and would you be qualified to take such a service?'

Burke let out a long breath while he

thought desperately. How much did this man know? And who had told him? Who had dropped him in the mire? Could it really have been Dolly's mother? More likely Don or Sid.

He said, 'I hope, Sergeant, that you haven't been talking to a certain Donald Wickham, because if so he has misled you. He'd say anything to get me into trouble, so if it was him you can forget it.' When the sergeant made no answer, Burke stumbled on. 'Never have got along with the man. Or his brother, come to that. I've known them a long time, but never got close to them. They're a funny pair, the brothers. Not to be trusted, if you know what I mean. Not what you'd call—'

'So you wouldn't pretend to marry someone if you weren't qualified to actually do so.'

'No. Wouldn't be right, would it?' He risked a smile.

'For a fee, perhaps?'

'Certainly not.' He was beginning to feel rather warm and hoped he wasn't sweating. Wiping his face with a handkerchief would be something of a giveaway. He knew from past experience that he had to play this very carefully because they were always looking for ways to call your bluff. Maybe he should try to brazen it out, he thought with a flicker

241

of hope. 'So can I go now? I've answered your questions, and I've warned you about that rat Wickham! You can't believe a word he says. Born troublemaker, he is.' He stood up.

The sergeant smiled. 'Sit down, Mr Burke. For your information, the person who alleges that you performed a fake wedding ceremony is a Mrs May Ellerway. Mother of a certain Jenny Ellerway. Name ring a bell, does it?'

He frowned. 'Ellerway? No. I don't reckon so.' That was best, he told himself. Act ignorant. Admit to nothing. They only had Mrs Ellerway's word for it ... unless she'd seen the marriage lines he'd produced. She may have taken them to show the police. Damn! That was what happened when you tried to do someone a favour. His attempt to please young Dolly just might prove his undoing. Swallowing, he found his throat dry. This wasn't looking good at all.

Uninvited memories of the prison crowded into his mind. Wash up in cold water, first thing in the morning in that dreary place crowded with evil-minded men ... emptying the slop buckets ... trudging round the exercise yard – not to mention the food which he hated, except for sago pudding, which he always enjoyed. He sighed.

'So you admit to knowing the Wickham brothers?' The sergeant was staring at him, his eyes narrowed. Before he could answer, another man entered the room dressed in civilian clothes and this gave Burke his first jolt of real fear. The sergeant stood up. 'This is DC Berry. A detective. He wants to ask you a few questions about a certain jeweller's shop. Glazers. Ring a bell, does it?'

'No!' Burke said hoarsely. 'It does not ring a bell!'

'Well, we'll come back to this marriage business later, Mr Burke.' The sergeant grinned at his colleague and said, 'He's all yours!'

As the detective sat down in the vacated chair, the sergeant leaned forward with both hands flat on the table. 'It's like this,' he told Burke. 'You're in deep trouble, Mr Burke, but you can save your skin if you're clever enough. You tell DC Berry all about the robbery, including the assault with a pistol on an innocent man, and we'll forget all about fraudulent wedding ceremonies and we might – I say *might* – recommend you for a lighter sentence.'

'Lighter sentence for what?' He tried to look puzzled.

'For driving the getaway car. That's what I heard, Mr Burke.'

Burke frowned. 'Don't know anything about a getaway car. Never heard of any of it. I'm innocent.' He looked from the sergeant to the detective, who were both grinning. 'What? I know the law. Innocent until proved guilty.'

The sergeant left the room, and the detective said wearily, 'If it takes all day and all night, Mr Burke, I'll get the truth out of you. We've got Sidney Wickham locked up, and now we've got you. It won't be long before we catch up with Donald Wickham. Your luck's just run out, Mr Burke, and to tell you the truth I'm feeling pretty smug, in case you're interested – but I don't suppose you are!'

Burke realized suddenly that he was no longer sweating. Instead he was aware of a leaden feeling deep within him. Those blighters have ratted me out, he reflected, sick with disbelief. They've bloody well snookered me! God damn their eyes! He sat back in his chair and took a deep breath. It seemed there was no way out. If Sidney had been fingered he'd have said anything to get himself off the hook – but without much luck, seemingly, if the sergeant was telling the truth when he said Sidney was already locked up. And that stupid cow, Dolly's mother, sticking her oar in!

He shook his head unhappily. They'd done wrong by him so he'd damn well return the favour. He took a deep breath. 'Well, if you must know, it wasn't me killed that man,' he said firmly. 'I was outside, waiting for them in the car. All you can get me for was waiting in the car! It was Don Wickham who whacked him!'

At the reception desk Mrs Duggett was handing over a sooty-looking package. 'It's a gun,' she told the bored-looking desk sergeant who was rising reluctantly from his chair. 'Found it stuck up my chimney.'

'A gun!'

There was a gleam of interest now, she thought triumphantly. 'Probably been there for years by the look of it, so don't blame me. Blame one of my lodgers. I've had all sorts over the years.' She thought that was rather clever. She did not want to get poor Mr Burke into any trouble. 'I'm just being a responsible citizen, that's all. Doing my duty by handing it in to the police.' She smiled modestly.

He eyed it cautiously. 'Loaded, is it?'

'Don't ask me! I haven't touched it. Soon as I saw what it was I wrapped it up again double quick and brought it round here. You're welcome to it! I don't want things like that in my house. Might go off and kill me, and then where would I be? Planted six feet under!'

Mrs Duggett gave a little laugh and hoped she sounded innocent of any ill-doing. She had decided not to try and get rid of it in case she was caught in the act, and this way she hoped she would earn a little respect for her community spirit.

The desk sergeant reached for a ledger and dipped a pen into the inkwell. 'Better have some details,' he said, trying to hide his excitement.

This, she thought, was brightening up his morning.

'Name and address, please madam.'

Eleven

Dolly was up in the attic when the doorbell rang, and she decided to ignore it. She had come up to the attic to consider a plan she had for renting out the space, and now she was making a mental plan of the room as it could be, if a suitable lodger could be found. The idea of abandoning her first home as a married woman was painful to her, and taking in a lodger seemed to offer a way out of the dilemma.

'Even if I'm not truly married – if what that stupid Sid said is true,' she muttered bitterly. Her mother's discovery that Willis Burke was not a real reverend had been a bitter blow to her pride, but she had done her best to rise above the disaster – telling herself that poor Don had also been taken in by Burke's smooth talking. She had her child to consider, and rushing back home to her mother and sister was unthinkable. She had tasted a few days of independence and was not yet willing to give up her new life.

The bed could go against the right-hand wall, she decided, and would only be a single so a male lodger would be deterred from bringing home a woman. Maybe a tartan blanket would look cheerful. A bed there would leave a space under the far window for a table and chair, and to the right she could fit in a chest of drawers ... but there would have to be washing facilities and somewhere to cook – unless she offered meals.

'I could do that,' she said. 'Plain food, that is, but I needn't charge too much. Mrs Daye has a lodger.' Maybe she would call on her and ask for advice. She had the address somewhere...

The bell rang again – a prolonged and very determined buzz which sent her hurrying downstairs as fast as her pregnancy would allow.

She opened the door to a young policeman and groaned aloud. 'You lot again?' she snapped. 'I hear you've arrested my brother-in-law. Isn't that enough?'

'I'm afraid not, Mrs Wickham – or should I say Miss Ellerway?'

Dolly tried to close the door, but he put out a large boot to hold it open. Seeing her furious expression he held up a hand by way of an apology. 'Sorry, miss. I mean

248

Mrs. That is...'

'What d'you want, Constable? I'm busy.'

'You need to answer some questions. Can I come in or shall we go to the police station?'

She could see admiration in his eyes as he considered her blue eyes and blonde curls, and Dolly thought rapidly. 'Do you know anyone who's looking for a room to rent? Our attic's very nice, and there's a bit of a view over the rooftops. I could show you the room if you like. It isn't furnished yet, but it will look very nice.'

'Er ... not at the moment, but I could ask around. You could show me the room though – after you've answered the questions.'

Dolly hesitated, then agreed. They ended up in the front room, sitting either side of a fireplace full of last winter's ashes.

He studied his notebook, trying to phrase his first question so as not to antagonize her.

'We have reason to believe,' he said carefully, 'that your husband Donald Wickham might be a suspect in a murder investigation. Do you have anything to say?'

'Say?' She looked at him blankly. 'You're saying my husband murdered someone? No. It's impossible!'

'I'm afraid not. We are currently looking for him, Mrs Wickham. We are led to believe that he struck a man on the head during a raid on a London jeweller's, and unfortunately the man has since died. We believe—'

'I don't care what you believe, it's not him. It's not my husband. He wouldn't kill anyone. Why should he?'

'It is alleged it might have been an accident, but it's still manslaughter, even if it's not murder, and we need to talk to your husband. Do you know where he is?'

'No, I don't, except that he's away on business. He's a very successful salesman. You could ask his brother Sidney since you've got him in custody. Lord knows what *he's* supposed to have done.'

'He is also involved in the robbery.'

'Who is? I can't understand all this.'

'Sidney Wickham is also involved. The two of them entered the shop on—'

'You're talking through your hat!' Dolly protested. 'I know my husband better than you do, Constable.'

'But he talked you into a phoney wedding, didn't he? You didn't know him that well!'

Dolly blinked. 'He trusted Willis Burke, that's all. We'll have a proper wedding when he gets back and finds out what's happened.' Even as she suggested it, her heart told her it would never happen, and that particular knowledge introduced all sorts of doubts.

250

Despite her brave words she felt as though the ground was shifting beneath her feet.

Risking a glance at the young policeman, she wondered if she could appeal to his better nature – if he had one. She pulled at one of her blonde curls, twisting it around her finger as she fluttered her eyelashes. 'There must be a mistake, Constable,' she said softly. 'Sidney Wickham must be lying through his teeth. And why would he need to rob a bank? He's got a private income from his grandfather. Family money. He told me so himself. He was the favourite so—'

'Family money? Hogwash!' The sergeant grinned. 'He certainly pulled the wool over your eyes!'

But Dolly was not listening, as her thoughts had taken off in another direction. Abruptly forgetting her womanly wiles, she frowned. 'Who ratted on Sidney and Don? Because whoever it was, they lied! They must have done.'

'I'm not allowed to divulge information,' he said sternly, 'except to say it was a so-called friend. So to get back to business, *Miss Ellerway*, we now have two members of the gang in custody, and we understand your hus ... your fiancé, Donald Wickham, is the ringleader. Do you know his whereabouts – yes or no? I have to remind you that withholding information is an offence. You don't want to join them, do you?'

Inwardly, Dolly was seething. If what this policeman said was true then Don had tricked her into believing that they were married. That nice Mr Burke had been pretending – and Don had known it! Her mother had suggested as much earlier on, but Dolly had denied it, accusing her of stirring up trouble between husband and wife. How could she face her mother again – now that all this was happening? She herself had been more than satisfied with her marriage lines with the red sealing wax. Mavis had been so jealous, and Dolly had been so happy as Mrs Donald Wickham ... and now she felt stupid. Don must have been secretly laughing at her for being so trusting. And now her poor baby would be born on the wrong side of the blanket! Dolly felt like weeping, but the tears refused to flow. She stared at the policeman and sighed deeply.

He said, 'Look, I'm sorry about all this, but you have to answer my questions. Do you know where your husband is?'

She shook her head.

'Do you know when he is coming back?'

She shook her head again. Maybe never, she thought miserably.

'Has he given you any jewellery, Miss

Ellerway, and if so, do you still have it? We have a list of stolen items that—'

'He gave me a diamond ring and said I was never to take it off or it would break the marriage vows, but when he went off I thought he'd never find out so I let Sidney take it to get it valued for me.'

'Did he now? How kind of Sidney!' He rolled his eyes, grinning again. 'Can you describe the ring?'

'They call them solitaires because they just have one special stone. Solitary, you see. That means "one". Like solitary confinement in prison. One person in a cell.' She felt rather proud of that information as she watched him taking notes.

He glanced up at her. 'Trust me – you won't see that ring again.'

'But he's going to bring it—' She paused as her thoughts raced on uneasily.

'Exactly!' he said, not unkindly. 'Sidney Wickham is up before the courts any day now and won't be coming back home for years. He was identified by an honest pawn-broker. Stolen property, Miss Ellerway. That's what that ring was. You can bet on it!'

'But it's mine! It was my wedding ring!'she protested.

'I'm afraid not. It was never Donald Wickham's property because it was stolen, so he had no right to be giving it to you and his brother had no right to be trying to pawn it. Don't you see? You could be charged with receiving stolen goods, but I believe that you did not understand the true situation. The police are after the three perpetrators, not gullible womenfolk.'

Hurt by the slur, Dolly held back a bitter comment. Things were bad enough, she reasoned, without upsetting the police.

By the time the sergeant left, Dolly felt as though her whole life had been a total muddle. She stood on the doorstep and watched the policeman ride away on his bicycle and thought that nothing worse could possibly happen to her.

She was wrong.

'Mrs Wickham?' A large middle-aged man had approached her from the opposite direction. He looked what her mother called 'thuggish', with a square flat face under a mass of brown hair. As he drew alongside she smelt the whisky on his breath.

'Mrs Wickham?' he repeated.

'Not any longer.' She sighed.

'But you do live here, don't you? 'Cause if you do you owe three weeks' rent and the boss says "pay up" or sling your hook!' To emphasize the point he held out a large calloused hand.

Dolly thought about it dispassionately. Did she still *legally* live at number sixteen? It was the Wickhams' place, but what was the point if Don was gone, Lord knows where, and Sidney was arrested? Did she want to stay there on her own? Probably not. Could she afford to settle the rent arrears? No. But could she bear to go home to Ma and Mave and have them gloat over her misfortunes? Most definitely not.

'What's it to be?' he asked, scratching his matted hair.

His surly tone and total lack of interest depressed her. 'I was planning to rent out the attic,' she confided, but her hopes were fading. 'If I did then I could pay you the rent that's owed. Would he wait for a week or so?'

'Don't ask me, I only collect the cash.'

'I dare say I could ask him myself.'

He shrugged. 'And if you don't find a lodger you'll owe even more.'

Regretfully, Dolly saw the logic of that and surrendered the idea. 'Tell your boss I'll be gone by nightfall,' she told him, 'and tell him from me–' she folded her arms belligerently – 'that the corner of the front bedroom reeks of damp and the wallpaper's peeling off. The kitchen window frame is rotten – you can press your finger through it – and there's a thing like a smelly brown mushroom growing in the cupboard under the stairs. Perhaps he should spend some money on the place before it falls down around the next lodger's ears!'

His smile revealed neglected teeth. 'Perhaps if people like you paid their rent on time, he would.'

'Just tell him!' she snapped.

'Tell him yourself.'

There was no answer to that so Dolly went inside, slamming the door behind her, then went upstairs to pack her few belongings. By the time she had finished she knew exactly where she was going and set off with Lydia Daye's address clutched in her free hand.

Later that day Lydia was polishing the silver – a job she had been doing from childhood and greatly enjoyed. Sitting at the kitchen table in the same kitchen, with cloths and polishes to hand, she had earned approval from her mother for her diligence and always received a penny for her labours which she would spend in the sweet shop on the corner. Now she smiled. She had spent ages in the little shop, which smelled of aniseed balls and chocolate and marzipan and many other smells that she could not name.

At that time she had enjoyed the luxury of being adored by both her parents, and she clearly remembered her excitement when her mother announced that they would soon have an addition to the family as the stork would bring her a baby brother or sister. When he arrived, the baby was named Robert, but there the happy ending rested for a number of years until a third child brought about drastic changes. The new sister died soon after birth, and her mother died a few months later, allegedly from an infection aggravated by an excess of grief.

She glanced from the kitchen window and was reassured to see her father sitting in the garden, well wrapped up against a blustery wind. Beside him Adam played with a bubble pipe and a bowl of soapy water, sending the bubbles high into the air and running after them with squeals of excitement.

Lydia smiled wistfully. The scene brought back memories of her brother Robert when he was the same age and adored by all and sundry – which included Lydia. Her father had doted upon him, but Lydia had never resented the fact that, as Robert grew older, her father paid her less and less attention. The boy's death had been a devastating blow to everyone, but her father had been half out of his mind with sorrow and the pain of loss.

'That's done!' she exclaimed, resettling the cutlery in its velvet-lined box and closing the lid.

As she was returning it to the dresser, she heard someone rapping on the back door. Opening it she found Adam pointing round the side of the house.

'There's a lady,' he told her.

'A lady? What do you mean, dear?'

'She's sitting on the step. And she's got bundles and things.'

'On *our* step? Surely not!'

Only half believing him, Lydia followed him round the side of the house and saw Dolly Wickham on the bottom step, lolling against the door, fanning herself with her hand.

'Mrs Wickham? I mean, Dolly. What brings you here?' She reached out a hand, and Dolly grasped it gratefully and allowed herself to be helped to her feet. She was red-faced and breathless from the exertion of her long walk.

'I'm sorry to bother you...' she began, one hand clutching her side. 'It's further than I thought.'

Puzzled by her unexpected visitor, Lydia picked up her bags and helped her round the side of the house and into the kitchen, with Adam prancing along beside them. Once inside the kitchen she refilled the kettle and set it on the stove, and then led her visitor into the front room where they could rest and talk in comfort.

Adam rushed to fetch the kitten and show him off to their visitor, who made admiring noises.

Lydia said, 'Find a little ball and play with Sooty, Adam. I have to talk to Mrs Wickham.' Presumably, Dolly's visit was something to do with the PSD, she thought, intrigued and suddenly hopeful.

For a few moments they discussed Dolly's health and that of the unborn child, but as soon as they were sipping their tea, Dolly dropped her bombshell.

'It's my husband,' she told Lydia. 'He's only skipped off and left me.'

'Left you? But Dolly, you've only just been married!' Lydia watched a series of emotions flit across Dolly's face. 'And the baby's coming soon. Is he quite mad?'

Dolly blew on her tea and sipped it cautiously. 'It gets worse,' she offered.

'How could it be any worse?'

'The police are after him, saying he's robbed a shop in London. Him and some other men. Three of them.' She averted her eyes as she spoke.

So this was nothing to do with the PSD, thought Lydia, disappointed. She said, 'And do you believe the police? It sounds quite

259

extraordinary to me.'

'And me! It sounds blooming ridiculous, but they've got the other two men, so they say, and they've blown the gaff on Don.' Her voice shook a little, and she helped herself to another spoonful of sugar and stirred vigorously as if she felt the need for a little more energy. 'So my husband is a thief, and he's wanted by the police!'

Lydia watched her curiously. How on earth, she wondered, could Dolly sit there reciting this terrible story without bursting into tears? If she were in Dolly's shoes she would be totally devastated and quite beyond comfort ... Unless Dolly was making it all up as a way to elicit pity – and possibly a little cash! Was this alleged betrayal simply a scam? The idea was an unpleasant one, and Lydia thrust it to the back of her mind. Bad things happened. She was usually a good judge of people, and she felt she could trust this brave little woman. At least, for the moment, she would give her the benefit of the doubt.

'They never even paid the rent!' Dolly told her. 'Three weeks was owing, and I didn't have the money so...' She shrugged, almost spilling what was left of her tea. 'So I had to get out. And I thought, this is all wrong! About my husband, I mean. It can't be true

... Although Don's not been back and that's a bit suspicious, don't you think? And that rotten Sidney took the ring and didn't bring it back and the sergeant said I could be arrested for wearing a ring that was stolen property!'

Lydia was revising her opinion. This sounded too complicated to be a pretence. And somewhere in Dolly's story she vaguely sensed there were unfathomable, uncomfortable echoes with her own situation. She stared at Dolly, frowning and listening intently.

'Who are these other two men?' she asked at last.

'One's his brother Sid. The other's the reverend who married us. His name's Willis Burke. They reckon he drove the getaway car after the robbery.' Seeing the expression on Lydia's face, Dolly nodded. 'Yes. He's the reverend – the man who married me and Don ... but the police reckon he was a fraud and me and Don aren't properly wed after all – although the captains of ships can marry people and so can the blacksmith at Gretna Green so why can't Mr Burke? He was a really nice man, and he gave me some violets and ... everything.'

'So are you going back to live with your mother?'

'No. I hate her. She's the one went round to the police about my wedding and got poor Mr Burke into trouble.'

'I expect she was trying to help you, wasn't she? To stop him from cheating you.'

'You don't know her like I do. She's always hated poor Don, and she was trying to get at him. To prove she was right! If she thinks I'm going to go crawling back she's—' She stopped suddenly, peering past Lydia. 'Is that your wedding?'

'Yes.' Lydia handed her the photograph in its silver frame.

Dolly smiled. 'Pretty dress! What colour was it?'

'A pale violet with pale-brown lace collar and cuffs.'

'Lovely!' She smiled. 'You'd look nice in violet. I had a cream skirt and jacket with those leg of mutton sleeves. I looked a treat with a white straw hat, although I say so meself. My ma always says you shouldn't blow your own trumpet! I wish *I'd* had a photo taken, but Don said we couldn't because it was a very private ceremony.' She studied the photograph, particularly the groom. 'I like your husband. He reminds me a lot of Don. Nice and tall. I like tall men. I know short men are nice, too, but I like to look up at Don. I used to think of him as my tall, dark stranger, although he wasn't a stranger. We grew up on opposite sides of the street!'

She handed back the photograph, and as she did so her face fell. 'The police said he hit a man and the man died and that makes Don a sort of murderer, even though he didn't mean it. That's why he's disappeared and I want him to come back but then they'll catch him and might hang him so in a way I have to hope he doesn't.' She put a hand over her belly. 'How could he run off without even waiting to see his baby? It's not natural.' Her eyes suddenly misted over. 'He should have taken us with him!'

Adam had followed the kitten into the kitchen, but now he returned. 'Where's Grandpapa?' he asked.

'He's in the garden.'

'No he isn't. I looked.'

There was a brief pause before his words registered, and then Lydia sprang to her feet with a cry of alarm. 'Run upstairs, Adam, and see if he's there!' She rushed to the front door and glanced up and down the road. There was no sign of her father.

Dolly had followed her to the front door as Lydia turned.

'He's wandered off again!' she cried. 'Oh Lord! It's my own fault. I got distracted and

263

forgot to keep an eye on him.'

Adam came downstairs shaking his head. 'He's not there, Mama.'

'And you looked in the bathroom and the bedrooms?'

'Yes, but he's not there.'

'Then I'll have to go after him.' Confused and beginning to panic, she looked at Dolly. Every moment she hesitated would take her father further from her and into possible danger. 'Can you wait here until I get back? I can go faster without Adam.' She turned to her son. 'Will you wait here with Auntie Dolly?'

He nodded.

Dolly smiled at him. 'I know a story about a teddy bear and a kitten called Sooty. Would you like to hear it?'

'Ooh yes!' He checked himself. 'I mean, yes please!'

'Come along then, Adam. There's plenty of room on my lap.' She winked at Lydia. 'He can share the space with *my* young'un!'

Lydia hesitated, weighing up her options. Dolly would take care of him, she decided, and Adam had taken to her. John would have a fit if he knew she was leaving their son with someone she hardly knew – but then John had abruptly disappeared from their lives with little or no explanation, leaving her with sole responsibility. He was in no position to criticize her decision, she told herself firmly.

'I'll be back as soon as I can,' she promised, and without bothering with a jacket she closed the front door behind her and, turning right in case her father was heading for the paper shop, she began to run along the road.

Adam watched his mother leave with obvious trepidation, but Dolly's story soon caught his imagination and he listened enthralled.

'...So the teddy bear said to himself, "I'm going to run away into the big wide world and see all the birds and animals"...'

'And the cows?' Adam added helpfully.

'*And* the cows and pigs and...'

'And the dogs?'

'Oh yes! The dogs, too. We mustn't forget them, must we? And the kittens...'

Dolly watched the little boy's face and tried to imagine that this was her own son and that everything was all right again and Don would be home for his supper of mutton stew and dumplings which she had cooked for them and then...

'What about white mice, Auntie Dolly?'

'Oh yes! Clever boy! How could I forget them?'

The story trailed on and on, held up by a multitude of interruptions, and Dolly's concentration wavered. She picked up the photograph of Lydia's wedding and stared at the husband. The mysterious John Daye who was not a spy but something very like a spy ...The likeness was astonishing, she thought. He could be Don's long lost brother! Her mouth twisted a little, and she sighed enviously. He and Lydia had obviously had a proper wedding.

'Auntie Dolly!' Adam prompted.

'Sorry, dear. I was looking at your ma and pa's wedding picture.'

'Papa has gone away and we don't know where he is but when he does come back he'll bring me a present but I mustn't ask about him any more because it makes Mama cry.'

'Oh dear! Poor Mama!' Dolly felt a rush of solidarity with the unfortunate Lydia Daye, but then an idea entered her head which was so monstrous that it made her voice falter and her head swim. Desperate and fearful, Dolly tried to hold out against the suspicion, but finally, cold with shock, she surrendered to the hateful possibility. Adam's father and the father of her unborn child could be one and the same. Was it...? She began to shake her head. No, she thought. I won't even think it … but somehow she was going to have to put the idea to Lydia.

'Auntie Dolly?'

'Yes, dear?' She looked down into his innocent eyes and saw the bleak future for all of them.

'What happens next?'

What indeed?

By the time Lydia reached the paper shop the full extent of her troubles had dawned on her also, and she was in no state to argue the finer points with her father and another man who were arguing heatedly over who had reached first for the last copy of *The Times*. Mr Wright was trying to calm matters, but a Mr Williams was insisting that Lydia's father had snatched the paper from him and George was denying it, insisting that Mr Williams was a cad and ought to be ashamed of himself.

Several other customers were watching the argument with interest, and an urchin child was taking his chance to fill his pockets with sweets before slipping out of the shop.

Without bothering about the niceties, Lydia snatched the paper from her father, handed it back to Mr Williams and dragged her father out of the shop on to the pavement.

'Don't look at me like that!' she told him through gritted teeth. 'And forget about *The Times*! We have trouble with a capital T, Father, so not another word. You are coming home with me. Now!'

To her relief he did not argue, but allowed himself to be led along with only a brief backward glance. He had been enjoying the little scrap, but Lydia was Lydia and would never understand the workings of a man's heart. Mr Williams was an obnoxious little squealer, with his fancy tweed suit and silly little spectacles, and George had longed to thwack him around the shoulders with the rolled up *Times*.

After a couple of hundred yards George stopped abruptly. 'So what has happened?' he asked. 'Why are you behaving like a shrew?'

She faced him with an expression he could not read but which sent a shiver down his spine. Trouble with a capital T. That was what she had said.

'If you think I am going to tell you in the middle of the street,' she began hotly, grabbing his arm, 'you're wrong!'

He looked into her white face and saw the strain in her eyes and felt the first stirring of deeper unease. 'I am not going a step further until I know what has happened,' he told her, 'and if you try to drag me home people will think you're kidnapping me!'

For a moment they stared at each other, and then Lydia said, 'When I tell you, you'll wish you were at home.'

'So be it!'

She hesitated as a woman walked past pushing a pram, then she said simply, 'I think Don has betrayed me ... with another woman.'

George drew in a sharp breath and struggled to remain focused. He said shakily, 'I wouldn't put it past him.'

'Dolly Wickham!'

He nodded.

'And if I'm right then, Father ... he is wanted by the police.'

A child ran past with a hoop.

She said, 'For theft and ... for assaulting someone who has died from the injuries.'

'He could hang!'

'Oh God!'

'When did you find out all this, Lydia?'

'I think it was beginning to dawn on me when Dolly was looking so closely at our wedding photograph, and I realized that if the letters I sent to her home were read and answered then John must have been there and ... and her husband goes away when mine goes away and ... and the rings and the pearls ... It was Glazers, the jeweller's, you see!' She drew a long, painful breath. 'What do you think, Father? Am I right? Could this really be happening?'

George put an arm round her waist, and she slumped against him. He asked, 'Did she know? Dolly Wickham – did she know he was already married?'

'I think not.'

'So he has betrayed her, too. Poor woman.' He tightened his arm round her as a young man walked towards them.

Sensing a possible problem the man paused, hesitating, regarding them suspiciously. Then to Lydia he said, 'You all right, miss? This man annoying you, is he?'

'No, no! Thank you for asking, but he's my father.'

George said stiffly, 'My daughter is feeling unwell. A little faint. I'll be taking her home as soon as she feels able to walk.'

If I ever do, Lydia thought with a touch of hysteria. I may never feel able to do anything ever again! This might be the straw that breaks the camel's back!

The young man looked from George to Lydia with an unspoken question. Lydia forced a smile. 'It's true. He is my father. I'm in no trouble.' But that was a lie, she thought. She was in very serious trouble, but

270

her father was not the problem – her husband was. 'But I appreciate your concern,' she added.

He gave a brief nod, touched the brim of his hat, said, 'Then I hope you feel better soon,' and walked on.

Silently, they watched him go. He turned back to give them a final cursory glance, then continued on his way, apparently satisfied.

George returned at once to their discussion. 'Are you going to tell Dolly Wickham? It will be a terrible shock for her, especially in her condition.'

Carefully, Lydia eased herself upright, taking her weight on her own two feet and finding that she was just about in control. 'We'll have to talk,' she said, 'but she's not stupid. She was looking very closely at my wedding photograph, and I suspect that, like me, she's already put two and two together.'

George tucked her arm in his, and they moved slowly in the direction of home. Still shocked by her recent discovery her steps faltered, and she felt like a hospital patient who has been given less than a month to live.

George said grimly, 'I'd like to get my hands on that bounder. I'd wring his damned neck with my bare hands!'

'He's Adam's father, remember.' She made

the protest from habit.

'I don't care who or what he is!' George replied hotly. 'So don't let yourself pity him, Liddy, and don't make excuses for him. You have to face facts, and you might as well start now. John Daye is an out and out bounder!'

'But he's still my husband.'

'More's the pity! Don't expect me to make allowances for him because I won't listen. We have to face a dreadful truth. John Daye has ruined our lives, and I want him to pay for it. Hanging would be too good for him!'

Twelve

As they approached the front door it was opened by Dolly and an excited Adam who immediately began to tell Lydia all about Sooty and the teddy bear, but after she had kissed him she suggested that George and Adam went into the front room.

'You can do a puzzle,' she told them, 'while I talk with Auntie Dolly in the kitchen.'

Once in the kitchen she closed the door, took a deep breath and faced her visitor.

Dolly, pale with a spot of colour on each cheek, held up her hand. 'You don't need to say it,' she said. 'I know! I've worked it out. I know about my husband and yours.'

'They're one and the same!'

'Yes. Two sides of the coin.'

'It's unbelievable, but...' Lydia shook her head. 'There is no other explanation.'

'I don't know what to feel,' said Dolly. 'It doesn't feel real. How could he do this?'

'I know. I love John and hate him at the same time.'

They regarded each other helplessly, and then Lydia stepped forward and put her arms round Dolly and they clung together, dry-eyed.

Dolly drew back at last and sank down on to a chair, and Lydia noticed that the kettle was boiling and that two mugs waited on the table. She made the tea in silence, adding a cup and saucer for her father and a glass of milk for Adam, both of which she carried into the front room. When she returned she said, 'Father knows. He wasn't surprised. Took it rather well, in fact.'

'But he'll be worrying inside.'

'Yes. Would you like a biscuit?'

'I couldn't.' Dolly sighed. 'I feel a bit sick. It's the shock ... Your son's a wonderful little chap. At least you've got him.' Her voice shook.

'You'll have a child soon, Dolly.'

'I wish I wasn't.'

'Oh, don't say that! Whatever his father has done, it's not the baby's fault.'

Despair was settling over them both like a cloud.

'He's been trouble all his life,' Dolly admitted. 'Pinching stuff from the shops, breaking windows, fighting. Ma used to say he should move into the police station – he spent so much time there. She was always warning

274

me and Mave about him, and then what do I do? I fall for him and get myself knocked up with his baby! What does that make me?'

'Did you really love him?' Lydia did not know which answer she was hoping for.

'I suppose so. He's got that air about him. Devil may care! He's always been exciting.' She stirred her tea and picked out a stray tea leaf. 'At least you were properly married. Weren't you? In a church, I mean?'

'Yes, but he said his name was John Daye, so if it isn't ... If it's Donald Wickham then I simply don't know where I stand!' She sighed heavily, one hand to her chest, which had started to ache. 'I almost wish that Mr Phipps had stayed out of it all. It all started when he offered to come to your house and try to find out about the PSD. It all seemed to go wrong after that.'

Dolly rolled her eyes. 'I expect he meant well, although you can never trust a copper!'

'Looking back I can see what was happening. The money was coming from the robberies, and he let me think he was doing his duty for the country. That he was a hero. And I trusted him.'

'So did I, but I should have known better! I grew up opposite the family. They were always trouble. His mother got the sack for stealing from the lady where she did the cleaning. His pa ran off years ago and left them.'

'Do you think circumstances are a good enough excuse?'

'Not really, but...' She shrugged. 'Well, you know ... setting his sons a bad example.'

Lydia bridled at the suggestion. 'I certainly don't assume that Adam is going to follow in his father's footsteps!' She was mortified to hear her voice rising and made a conscious effort to lower it. 'I shall make sure Adam never knows. I shall keep the truth from him. Pretend that John died in an accident or of an illness. That will be the kindest thing I could do for the poor little man. How could I let him grow up knowing his father was a thief and a murderer?'

It was Dolly's turn to protest. 'Don's not a true murderer because he didn't mean to kill that man. It's not as if he shot him. They say it was an accident. The man was hit on the head and fell and hit his head again on the floor and—'

'Exactly. He was hit on the head – by John! No one has suggested it was self-defence. Just a foolish man trying to be a hero.'

'But he wasn't shot or stabbed. It was an *accident*.'

'Maybe, maybe not ... but he's still very dead, poor man, and John's to blame. If they

276

hadn't been robbing the shop...'

Dolly frowned in an effort to solve yet another problem thrown up by the circumstances. 'I shall have to tell my son the truth because round where I live everyone knows everyone else's business and he'll find out from his school mates. Sure to!'

'You could move away from there,' Lydia suggested. 'Anyway, you might have a girl. Things are a bit different for girls.' She saw Dolly's expression change. 'What is it?'

'I've just realized – they'll be related. Our children!'

'Related? Oh no!' Taken aback by the idea, Lydia had allowed her dismay to show and now, not wishing to hurt Dolly, hastily tried to lessen any offence she might have caused. 'You're right, of course. Half brothers ... or is it step brothers?'

At that moment Adam came into the kitchen looking troubled. 'Grandpapa is sad,' he announced. 'He says he's not crying, but he is!'

'Oh, Adam!' She jumped to her feet. 'Excuse me, Dolly.'

In the front room she found her father weeping silently and threw her arms around him. 'You're tired, Father. Come up to your bedroom for a rest, and I'll make you some porridge with cream and sugar the way you

277

like it. You always find that comforting.' She helped him, unprotesting, from the chair, and they made their way up the stairs to his room, where she took off his shoes and jacket and helped him into his favourite armchair beside the window.

'I'm useless!' he complained suddenly. 'Just a useless old man. What good can I do for you, eh, Liddy?' He accepted the handkerchief she found in his top drawer. 'Just when you need me I'm utterly useless.'

'No, Father! That's not true. Just having you around is a great help to me. To both of us. And Adam adores you.'

He shook his head. 'I wish that were so, but I sometimes think he's afraid of me. He doesn't understand me, and I can't blame him. I don't understand myself half the time!'

Fresh tears filled his eyes, and Lydia searched for some way to convince him. 'We both love you...' she began.

'But I'm a liability! Just an extra worry for you. Don't think I don't know!'

'Father! Please listen to me and don't cry any more. You are very important to me and to Adam. You know how much he loves you. And I need you. Without John I shall be so grateful for your company. You are *not* a liability.'

'But I do silly things. I worry you. I wander off. If only Robert were here. He's a sensible young man. He'd be a great help.'

Lydia let it pass. She closed her eyes and leaned down to kiss the top of her father's head. 'I won't listen to another word!' she said, in an attempt to sound brisk and purposeful. 'You rest in this chair until I bring up your porridge, and no more tears and no more worries. I think we still have some demerara sugar, and I know you prefer that.' She forced a smile. 'My shoulders are broader than you think, Father. We'll help each other through this. I'm quite determined.' She took the damp handkerchief and found a replacement. 'You'll see. We'll manage without my wretched husband. You were right about him all along, but now we know the worst and we can survive.'

He caught her hand and squeezed it. 'You're a good girl, Liddy. You don't deserve all this trouble.'

She was halfway to the door when he said, 'That other poor woman! His other wife. What will she do now?'

'I don't know, Father. We're talking it over at the moment.' And she's not his 'other wife', she argued inwardly. They were never married ... But there was the baby, she conceded unwillingly, so she did have some claim on him.

As she made her way downstairs, Lydia, for the first time, felt a first real flash of anger towards her husband and found, to her surprise, that it was so much easier to bear than grief.

Later that night, Leonard Phipps laid down his pen and reread what he had said to his mother in the letter. He had told her the situation with some reluctance because he knew it would worry her, but a change of address would need an explanation. He had started and ended with the good news, so hopefully she would be distracted from the less welcome news in the middle:

Dear Mama, I hope this finds you reasonably well. I am hale and hearty with an appetite to match so do not worry that I am not being fed properly.

You will be pleased to hear that I have been recommended for early promotion, so as soon as there is a vacancy I shall become a sergeant. Now that is something you can boast about when Mrs Thwaite comes to tea! I am delighted.

Those enquiries I told you about last time I wrote led to further investigations which tied in with the robbery at Glazers in Oxford

Street. As usual one thing led to another and has resulted in two arrests – one of the robbers, a man named Sidney Wickham, and one Willis Burke, who was the driver of the car in which they escaped! They are still searching for the third man – the one who caused the death of an innocent shopper. He is still on the run, but we are hopeful of bringing him to justice also.

The unfortunate aspect of this, however, puts me in a difficult position because the wanted man is no other than Mrs Daye's husband! Worse still, the wretch is also involved with another woman, who is expecting a child by him. Hard to believe, is it not, Mama, but they say truth is stranger than fiction!

As soon as poor Mrs Daye recovers from the shock she has had, she will at some stage realize the significance of my unwitting role in this mess, and she will almost certainly want me out of her house. I cannot find it in my heart to blame her. I regret that I have inadvertently caused her so much pain and feel, quite illogically, that I have betrayed her trust. It was necessary, but it saddens me. I am already looking for accommodation elsewhere.

To end on a cheerful note, I have been granted a weekend's leave the week after next *so will travel up on the late train Friday and return Sunday. What a lot we shall have to talk about!*

Sighing, he signed off in the usual way and slipped the letter into an envelope.

That night Lydia lay in bed as the church clock struck two, as wide awake as when she first scrambled between the sheets. She thought about those around her – Adam fast asleep, clutching his teddy bear; her father, tossing restlessly in the room on her right; Mr Phipps, silent in his room next to her father.

And upstairs in the attic on a makeshift bed – Dolly, crying herself to sleep. Lydia had felt quite unable to send her away, knowing that she had nowhere to go since she refused to forgive her mother for her 'treachery'.

Lydia's confusion was total, and for the first time in her life she had no idea what to do next. Her entire life and its familiar routines had been snatched away, not only by John's defection, but also by his crime, and she dared not dwell on the horrors that awaited her family when, if, he was brought to trial and possibly hanged.

'You're out of your depth, Lydia!' she told

herself. The security of a home and a husband who paid the bills had vanished and,
unless her father had some money tucked
away, they had nothing coming in except the
small amount she earned from Mr Phipps'
occupation of their spare room.

This line of thinking was abruptly interrupted by a new thought which made her
gasp with horror. Was Dolly the only one? Or
had John 'married' anyone else?

'No!' she whispered. 'I mustn't think that
way. I'm just torturing myself.'

She supposed that Dolly was also wide
awake and pondering her future and that of
John's other child – a future that seemed
bound inevitably with that of her and Adam.

'Where *are* you, John?' she muttered, and
then made a new and devastating discovery.
They could never be together again the way
it was, even if he somehow escaped the arms
of the law, because his betrayal had been
complete. Too many lies had slipped glibly
from his tongue! He had lied to her about
everything, painting himself as a man she
could admire and trust; painting their life
together as something beautiful. Now she
knew that it had all been a deliberate sham –
and shabby, to boot.

'So how will we live?' she asked, staring up
into the darkness. Perhaps they could sell the

house and rent something much smaller and live off the remainder until it ran out. But what then? And there was the question of her father. He would never improve, but might well deteriorate. The idea of hiring a nurse to care for him when it became necessary was now an impossibility. She would be tied to the house, looking after him, so could hardly find herself a little job – and anyway, what could she do? Serve in a shop, perhaps? Write letters for London's illiterates? Work in an office? Scrub floors...?

Lydia did not hear the clock strike three, for she had slipped into a troubled sleep, temporarily leaving her worries behind her. But those same fears and dilemmas would be waiting for her when she awoke from her dreams to face the nightmare of the new day.

Dolly woke up just as it was getting light and was surprised to see George Meecham standing by her bed in his pyjamas. 'What is it?' she demanded, sitting up hastily. 'What do you want?' She fumbled on the bedside table for the matches and lit her candle.

He leaned down to peer at her. 'You're not Robert!' he said. 'Where's Robert?'

'He's away for a few days,' she invented, unwilling to enter into a long discussion. Better to go along with him, she thought.

'Go back to bed, Mr Meecham, or you'll catch a chill.' She pulled the bedclothes up around her neck. 'It's a cold night,' she lied. 'Go back to bed and in the morning we'll—'

'He never stays out this late.' George hesitated. 'This is his room, you see. Who are you?'

'I'm Dolly Wickham, a friend of your daughter Lydia. She knows I'm here. She said I can stay until tomorrow, and then I'll be looking for somewhere else.'

'Ah! I see.' He looked perplexed. 'So he's not lost then. Robert? He's not ... he hasn't wandered off?'

'No.' She smiled. 'He's quite safe. Now, you should go back to your own room, Mr Meecham, and get back into bed. We'll talk about it tomorrow.'

'Will we? Right. What did you say your name was? Dotty?'

'Dolly.'

'Ah! Well, goodnight, Dolly.' Obediently, he turned to go, and when he had left the room she slid from the bed and ran after him to make sure he had indeed gone back to bed. Once he was safely tucked up she crept back to her own bed, blew out the candle and climbed back into the comfort of the bedclothes. She didn't envy Lydia her future, with a child to bring up, an income to earn and a confused old man to look after.

'You're going to have your work cut out!' she muttered. 'But then so am I. Donald Wickham alias John Daye, has left us both on a very sticky wicket!' She closed her eyes, but immediately opened them to add, 'Damn him to hell!' and then cried herself to sleep.

When Dolly left the house next morning she heard Lydia stirring in her room and Adam calling to his mother from his bedroom. She presumed that the old man was still asleep and smiled with satisfaction. They would all assume that she was still asleep also. She hoped that by the time they realized she was missing she would be back and would have succeeded in her rather daring plan.

She presented herself at the reception desk of the local police station and said, 'My name's Jenny Ellerway, and I need to talk to someone in authority.'

'That's me then. Constable Bluitt at your service.' He smiled at her.

'It's about Mr Sidney Wickham,' she told him.

He was looking at her swelling belly, but made no comment.

He was very young, she noted, and hope-

286

fully still gullible. Dolly shook her head. 'I'm his sister-in-law,' she told him. 'They say he's been found guilty and sent down. I need to talk to him.'

'Hard luck, miss – or should I say missus?' She gave him a sharp look, and he hurriedly continued: 'He went before the magistrate a day or two back and is being transferred today to Strangeways Prison to join his partner in crime, Willis Burke. From here on in your Sid Wickham will be known as Prisoner 7221, and he's currently tucked up in his cell–' he jerked his thumb towards a long corridor – 'waiting for his breakfast of cold porridge and weak tea. A taste of things to come, if you'll pardon the pun!'

Dolly had no idea what a pun was so let it pass without comment. 'His ma's just died,' she said, hastily adjusting her expression. 'She sent me a message to him, to say "goodbye". I was wondering if I could just pass it on to him in person because it was her last request, poor old dear.' She took out a handkerchief and dabbed at her eyes

'Pass on a personal message? Certainly not!' He looked pleased by this opportunity to show the power of his position. 'Strictly against the rules.'

Dolly sized him up. He was about twenty, with blue eyes, nice fair hair, middle parting, trying to grow a moustache. Too young to be married, she decided, but might be courting.

'I could make it worth your while,' she whispered. 'Not with money but – you know. No one would ever know except the two of us.' She smiled from beneath her lashes and twiddled with a long blonde curl, winding it round her finger.

He looked suitably surprised, she thought and added, 'Just a kiss and a cuddle, nothing more, but most men wouldn't say no.'

'I don't know about that.' He hesitated. 'Not that I'm a married man or anything...'

He was flummoxed, she thought, and she could almost see his mind working. Almost hear the gears whirring! So where's the power now? she thought gleefully and said, 'How would you feel if it was your ma what had died?' When he still did not respond she gave a long sigh, glancing at the clock on the wall. 'Well, it was worth a try! Never mind, Constable. You're not the only pebble on the beach. What time do you go off duty, Constable Bluitt?'

Taken aback, he frowned. 'Two thirty, but what's it got to do with you?'

'Nothing to do with you, but your colleague might have more sense!' She smiled. 'I'll tell him you turned down the offer!'

Turning on her heel, Dolly was halfway to

the door when he called, 'Oi! Come back here! I didn't say no, did I?'

'But you didn't say yes.' Inwardly rejoicing, Dolly went back to the desk, trying to appear disinterested in his change of heart.

Casting a quick glance round the area to make sure they would not be overheard, he lowered his voice. 'Where and when?' he asked hoarsely.

'Ten o'clock tonight by the Fox and Hounds. There's an alley by the—'

'I know it! And you'll be there?'

She stiffened indignantly. 'You calling me a liar?'

'No! Course not! It's a deal then.' He reached for a key from the board behind him. 'Three minutes, that's all. I daren't risk any more. The custody sergeant will blow a gasket if he finds out!'

Inwardly rejoicing, Dolly followed him along the row of doors to the cell where Sidney was being held. All she had to do now was talk Prisoner 7221 into the rest of her plan.

Sidney looked up as footsteps approached in the corridor and came to a halt outside his cell. Was this his breakfast? Lumpy porridge and a mug of weak tea. Hardly something to look forward to. A key turned in the lock, and the door opened to reveal his sister-in-law and Constable Bluitt.

'What the...' he began.

But before the constable could speak, Dolly winked and said, 'Very bad news, I'm afraid, Sid!'

Dolly was pushed into the cell, and the constable said, 'Three minutes. I'll be back!' He locked the door when he left.

Sid said, 'What are you doing here?'

Dolly put a finger to her lips. 'I thought you'd like a visitor so I told him your ma had died. Make sure you look miserable after I go.'

Suddenly, he was beaming at her. 'I *shall* be miserable after you go! You're like a ray of sunshine, you are!'

'Stop smiling, Sid. You're supposed be getting bad news!'

He adjusted his expression and said, 'What news, if any, about Don?'

'None yet. So far, so good!'

'So there's no one at home.'

'Not even me because you two didn't pay the rent and I couldn't pay it because you went off with my ring. My wedding ring. And I know it's worth a lot and I want it back!'

'I don't know where it is!' He tried to look offended, but his mind was on other things.

Firstly, how pretty she was; secondly, how she was not really married to his brother; and thirdly, either Don would be on the run forever or else he'd be caught and banged up for years. So ... maybe Dolly was suddenly available.

'Don't even think about it!' Dolly told him, grinning.

'Think about what?'

'What you were thinking. I've had enough of the Wickham brothers, but we don't have time for all this nonsense! I've got a proposition for you, and if you don't agree I'll tell the police that you know where the ring is and they'll get it out of you. You'll have another black eye!'

He blustered briefly, but his heart was not in it. By the time Constable Bluitt returned, Dolly knew the truth.

'It was easier than I expected,' Dolly told Lydia while George and Adam were safely out of earshot, playing in the garden with the kitten. 'Poor old Sid! His eyes lit up when he saw me, but he wasn't so keen when I told him what I wanted.'

'Which was...?'

'Which was to know where he'd hidden my ring! He told the police he'd sold it, but I gave him more credit than that. More fool me. He'd sold it all right and left the money with a mate! Can you believe that?'

'Left it with someone? But he'll never see the money again!'

'Hard to believe, but Sid's stupid enough to do it. So we can kiss goodbye to the money. I could have strangled him.'

'What was it like in there? How did he seem?'

'They'd roughed him up a bit, but nothing out of the ordinary. A black eye and a missing tooth ... But I reckon he deserved that for tricking me into parting with my ring.'

'But it was stolen property!'

Dolly shrugged. 'Not by me! I didn't steal anything. Don *gave* it to me, and I didn't ask any questions. Anyway, I needed it more than Glazer's! They'll be getting the insurance. I've not got a penny to my name and...' She stopped for breath. 'Anyway, one thing's certain. The money's gone. I'll not see any of it. I was going to do a deal with him – I'd visit him in prison once a month...'

'Dolly! How could you? Visit a prison?'

'Why not?' Dolly shrugged. 'I'd have taken him cakes or sweets in return for half of the money. I'd have kept my part of the bargain – for me and the baby – but it wasn't to be.'

Lydia was shocked by Dolly's logic, but secretly full of admiration. In more ways than one, Dolly was a revelation.

Dolly gave her a scornful look. 'Wouldn't you do the same if they catch Don?'

'Have you forgotten, Dolly, that if they catch him he'll probably get the death penalty!'

'Oh Lord!' She put a hand to her mouth to hide her trembling lips.

After a silence, Lydia said, 'What about that constable? At ten o'clock by the Fox and Hounds...?' As soon as the words were out of her mouth she wished them unsaid, fascinated by the idea of the secret rendezvous, but actually reluctant to hear any further details.

'Oh, that.' Dolly, recovering, pulled herself together and tossed her head. 'I just shan't be there. He'll realize he's been had and serve him right! He's a policeman and should behave himself and not let himself be sweet-talked by pretty women! He's hardly going to tell anyone, is he?' She giggled. 'Being cheated by a silly little thing like me! If anyone found out he'd look a real mutt.'

'He'd probably get the sack!' Lydia was beginning to feel sorry for him.

'Serve him right.' Dolly shrugged.

Lydia allowed her mind to wander, and suddenly she narrowed her eyes. 'John told me years ago that his mother was dead. I wanted to meet her. That was obviously another of his lies.'

'Not really.' Dolly winked. 'It was *me* that lied. Mrs Wickham died years ago.'

That evening, after their meal, Leonard Phipps asked to speak to Lydia in private and, sensing a problem, Dolly quickly agreed to keep an ear open for Adam in case he awoke while Lydia and her lodger spoke in the front room.

They sat down, and Leonard cleared his throat nervously. 'It's not good news, I'm afraid,' he began. 'The unhappy fact is—'

'It's about my husband, isn't it?' Lydia clasped her hands against her chest. 'Please tell me straight, Mr Phipps.'

'I wish I didn't have to tell you this, but as a friend...'

She did not deny this, but waited impatiently for the bad news she knew would follow. How, in the circumstances, could the news be otherwise?

He leaned forward a little. 'Your husband was apprehended earlier today...'

'Oh God!' She swallowed convulsively.

'In the High Street in Durham.'

'Durham?' Lydia closed her eyes, trying to shut out the image of her husband, his hands manacled, being roughly manhandled by his triumphant captors. He would be broken … humiliated. Although he had caused her such heartbreak, the part of her that still loved him was appalled.

But Durham? What on earth was he doing in Durham, she wondered – unless he had friends there who might have been sheltering him. She said nothing, but her thoughts raced. So this moment signalled the end of everything – her marriage, John's freedom, her son's happy life. Life as I know it is at an end, she thought as she tried to slow her breathing. She felt cold and dizzy.

As though he had read her thoughts, Leonard said, 'He'd been living rough on the streets, sleeping in an alley...'

Lydia held up a shaking hand. 'Don't! I can't bear it!' Living rough on the streets? She tried to imagine her husband unshaven and in need of a wash. How he would have hated it. Poor John.

'He'd broken into a house soon after dawn – in search of food, presumably – but the household were roused by the noise and he fled up the stairs and climbed out of the window...'

Her eyes widened in horror as she pictured the scene, but at that moment the front-room door opened and her father put his head round the door to bid them goodnight.

'Thought I'd have an early night, Liddy,' he said.

They both said goodnight and waited until they heard his footsteps on the stairs. Liddy leaned back in the chair and put a hand to her head. 'Please go on,' she said faintly.

'I'm afraid it gets worse, Mrs Daye.' In halting tones he explained that there had been an accident. The wanted man had tried to escape by running across the rooftops with several policemen scrambling after him. 'One of the officers grabbed at his jacket and there was a scuffle and ... both men rolled down the roof and fell to the pavement. The officer was injured – two broken legs – but your husband ... I'm sorry, Mrs Daye, but he was killed.'

Lydia stared at him, breathless with shock. Killed! *Killed?* There must be some mistake, she told herself desperately. 'Mr Phipps, are you saying that my husband is *dead?*'

'I am. I'm so sorry. It was an accident. They were both taken to hospital, but your husband was pronounced dead on arrival. The injured sergeant may never walk properly again.'

'Poor man. How dreadful!' She tried to stand, but her legs failed her and she fell back in the chair.

He said, 'Your guest will need to know. She

was married to ... Well, not married, but involved.'

'I can't tell her!' Lydia panicked at the thought. 'You must do it. I have to lie down. I have to get up to my room and rest. Please...'

'I'll speak to her, but there is one more thing, Mrs Daye. In the circumstances – you being the wife of a known criminal – my superiors have said I must leave these premises. It's a compromising situation, you see. I hope you'll understand that I meant you, that is, I *mean* you, no ill-will. It's police policy.'

She barely grasped his meaning as she struggled to her feet, and so she made no reply. As she swayed he stood up and moved towards her, offering the support of his arm, but she shook her head. 'Don't! I can manage alone.'

As she crept slowly up the stairs the words rang in her head. *I can manage alone.* But could she, she wondered as she reached her room and threw herself on to the bed. Only God knows, she thought, but for Adam's sake, I shall have to try.

Thirteen

Dolly took one look at Leonard's face and jumped to her feet. 'It's bad news! Tell me. I have to know everything.'

Briefly, he explained the situation, watching her face, seeing her expression change as realization dawned on her.

She said, 'Hell and damnation!' then clapped a hand over her mouth.

'I'm sorry.'

'So you should be!' Dolly gave him a withering look. 'Hounding a man to his death!'

'He didn't have to go up on the roof,' Leonard protested. 'Because of him one of our officers has two broken legs and his career is ruined. Wickham didn't *have* to rob a shop either, so don't blame the police for doing their job.'

'I do blame you. You could have waited for him to come down.'

'If he'd earned an honest crust instead of turning to crime, he wouldn't been up on the roof in the first place!' Breathless and defensive, he faced Dolly angrily. 'And what about that man in the jeweller's shop? He died because of your so-called husband! Donald Wickham was no saint, believe you me!'

Shaken by his words, Dolly struggled to hold her ground. She folded her arms and spoke angrily, but inside she was trembling. 'I suppose you're satisfied now. You've ruined our lives, mine and Lydia's! I hope you're ashamed of yourself. All that snooping around and asking about the PSD. That was just a cover, wasn't it? You were really after the Wickhams!'

'I was doing my job, that's all. And I was trying to help Mrs Daye to trace her husband, who seemed to have disappeared. No one knew then that he was a professional thief. Mrs Daye thought he might be in danger on behalf of the government. It was a coincidence, that's all.'

'So you say!' She tossed her head, longing to sit down, but unwilling to let him see how deeply the news had affected her. 'And stop calling him Mr Daye. His name's Donald Wickham, not John Daye!' When he refused to be drawn, she said, 'What am I supposed to tell my child? His father died being chased by the police? That's going to sound very nice, that is!'

Leonard shrugged. 'He brought it on himself.' The truth was he felt truly sorry for the women, but he could not bring himself to say anything which might be construed as a criticism of the police force. Instead, he changed the subject. 'You'll be pleased to know I'm leaving these lodgings as soon as I've packed my things. I shall be sorry to leave. Everyone here has been very kind, but the station is finding me alternative lodgings.'

'The sooner the better!'

'I'll get on with my packing, then.'

As soon as he left the kitchen, Dolly sank down on to a chair. She put her hands on her belly protectively. 'Don't you fret,' she told the child. 'We'll be hunky dory, just the two of us. Your pa was a good man, but things went wrong for him.' She nodded approvingly. 'Yes. That's it. It was all very sad, but these things happen ... and he sent you his love and said be a good boy – or girl – and do what your ma tells you to do!' She rolled her eyes. 'And don't go falling off any roofs!' she added as she stood up and reached for the kettle.

First thing next morning Dolly set off to the paper shop with Adam and George, and while the former decided which sweets to spend his penny on, and George decided on a newspaper, she scanned the dozens of postcards on the notice board, in search of a job.

Cot For Sale, orlmost brand new. 1 shilling. Will Deliver.

Dolly thought it might be useful for when her child arrived, but then realized that she didn't have a spare shilling so looked further.

Window Cleaner. Fair prices. Up to first floor. Inquire at Number 3, Holden Street.

'Haven't got any windows!' she muttered.

Honest Cleaner needed. 1 hour daily. References required. Ask inside for details.

Frustrated, Dolly shook her head. She had decided to become a companion to a rich old lady, with accommodation for her and the child as part of the deal. She imagined herself on the way to the park, pushing the old soul in a bath chair with the child cheerfully trotting alongside. It might be a boy wearing a sailor suit. A girl would be dressed in frills with a lacy bonnet. The old lady would be a spinster with rheumatics but very sweet tempered with no family of her own and would take a shine to Dolly and the child and would die and leave them everything in her will. Inspired by this rosy picture, she pressed on with her search.

Another card, with fading ink and curling

301

corners, offered mongrel puppies for sale. Next to that, heavily pencilled, was a comparatively new card dated a week earlier:

Washing and irening collected and returnd same day.

'Same day? But suppose it rains?'

Slowly losing hope, Dolly read on. There was a second-hand perambulator on offer, cast-off clothing to fit a five- to six-year-old boy, a singing canary in a wicker cage, and a pair of blue blankets, slightly faded. Fascinating, she thought, but hardly helpful. Discouraged, Dolly sighed. None of these advertisements sounded as though they were written by rich old ladies, but maybe they advertised some other way.

George interrupted her investigation. 'We are on our way back, Dolly. Are you coming?'

Adam waved a raspberry lollipop to show her what he had spent his money on, and Dolly hesitated. Dare she let them out of her sight while she read the rest of the advertisements? Probably not, she decided and gave in gracefully.

'I've seen enough for today,' she told him, and the three of them set off towards home.

They were halfway there when it occurred to her that a rich but elderly and lonely old man would be almost as good as the sweet-tempered old woman.

Lydia had spent a sleepless night, dozing fitfully between long hours of worry about the future. At first the problems had appeared insurmountable, but she'd still hoped that gradually some kind of plan might form in her mind. Mr Phipps had left them, and she had stripped the bed and cleaned up the room – not that he had left it untidy, but because, since the recent revelations, she somehow felt the need to rid the house of a police presence. It had been humiliating to realize that now, in Leonard Phipps' eyes, she was no longer a respectable citizen, but the wife of a criminal. And in her own eyes John Daye's behaviour had lowered her in her own estimation and had sullied her family. Hopefully, her father had not realized the full significance of the events of the past few days, but he had said all along that John was not all he claimed to be. He had thought her husband a spy!

'And I thought Father was being paranoid! Love is certainly blind!' she whispered. And poor Leonard Phipps had had the thankless task of breaking her heart when he told her the truth. Yes. He'd had to go. She knew it was illogical, but she felt better now that the spare room was restored to its usual condition.

By morning Lydia had worked out a possible plan of action. It was far from ideal, but it might see them through the next few months – by which time Dolly's baby would be born and they could reconsider the future. First, however, she needed to gain her father's approval, so immediately after the midday meal she drew him into the garden for a private conversation.

'I'm wondering, Father,' she began hesitantly, 'whether or not we should offer Dolly the chance to live with us for a while – at least until she has her child. She seems to be without money or any means of support and appears to think she will get a job as a companion.'

'She has a family, doesn't she?'

'They are apparently at loggerheads.'

'She might get a job, you say, as a companion. Perhaps she will.'

'And perhaps she won't. At least, not in her present condition. If she were not ... in the family way she would stand a better chance. Who would want to choose a companion who is about to ... to become a mother, with all the disruption that will cause?'

Her father paused to de-head three of the nearest roses. Having picked them, he examined the faded petals, lost interest and dropped them on to the ground. 'She seems a nice enough woman,' he said mildly.

'I think she is, and she has also suffered at the hands of John or Don or whatever his name is. Was,' she corrected herself. Realizing that she sounded like a shrew, she said, 'I'm sorry, Father, but I'm finding it very hard to forgive my husband for what he has done. I try not to be bitter for Adam's sake – I am terrified for the future if he should ever find out the truth!'

'You are entitled to feel that way, Liddy. You must not be so hard on yourself.' He bent to pull up a few dandelion leaves which, for some reason best known to himself, he then put in his jacket pocket. 'The man deceived and betrayed you. That is an undeniable fact. He's an absolute bounder!'

'Was, Father. He's dead now.'

'Dead? Is that so?'

'I did tell you.' She took a deep breath. 'He fell from a rooftop.'

'Ah yes. So he did.'

'You were right about him. I should have listened to you from the start, but I was so...' She bit back the words, still afraid that her anger would make her say something she might regret.

'You loved him, my dear. We all make mistakes.' He glanced round the garden, eyes narrowed. 'Well, if he comes back here – if he sets a foot in this place again – he'll regret it! Spy or no spy, I'll throw the wretch out on his ear!'

'He won't, Father. Remember what I told you? He was killed trying to evade the law. He fell from a roof and was killed.'

'Killed? Good Lord!' He rapped his head with his knuckles. 'I can't seem to hold a sensible thought for more than five minutes!'

'So, Father, what do you think about asking Dolly to stay for a while. A few weeks or months, maybe? Shall we ask her?'

'By all means. Yes, indeed. You do what you think best.' He frowned. 'What's happened to the swing, Liddy? Robert's swing. I was thinking that Adam might like it. He'd like to have a swing. All children like to have a swing.'

Lydia sighed but forced a smile. 'I think the ropes wore out a long time ago, but...'

'And Robert has grown out of it.'

'Yes. We'll buy another one for Adam. That's a very good idea!'

George's face brightened at once. 'He'll like that.' Suddenly, he fished out of his pocket the already wilting dandelion leaves, dropped them on to the path and ground them with the sole of his shoe. 'Beastly things, weeds!' he said. 'I never could abide them.'

306

★ ★ ★

Without giving herself time to consider further, Lydia went to find Dolly and put the suggestion to her.

'You could have Mr Phipps' room,' she said. 'You wouldn't be a servant or anything like that because we couldn't pay you, but you could "live in"...'

Dolly's eyes lit up at the offer, and she thought quickly. 'I could earn my keep, anyway. I could help you with Adam and your father, so that would take some of the strain off you. I was thinking of being a companion to someone rich, but it would be more fun here with you! And I love your little boy, and your father and I get along.' She grinned. 'So I'll say yes before you change your mind. And when the baby comes...'

'We'll deal with it together!'

They regarded each other warily, almost afraid to believe that this might solve most of their problems.

Dolly spoke first. 'So is Mr Phipps' room mine now?'

'Yes. The bed's made up. You can move right in.'

It almost seemed too easy, thought Lydia, always cautious. Nervously, she crossed her fingers. She said, 'It won't be all clear sailing. I'm sure things will go wrong sometimes.

They always do, but...'

'We'll get by!' Dolly laughed. 'What would Don say if he could see us now? He spent so much time and effort keeping the two of us apart, and instead he's brought us together!'

Lydia sighed. 'I'm trying not to think of him,' she confessed. 'I swing between hating him and loving him ... and most of all despising myself for being stupid enough to believe all his lies.'

'We were both tricked,' Dolly told her soberly. 'We trusted him because we loved him – and he betrayed us both. It's as simple as that.'

Epilogue

Tuesday morning, mid-November 1907

Dolly had taken seven-year-old Adam and little Clara to the park for an hour to give Lydia a quiet house in which to talk to the new doctor about her father's problems while George rested upstairs.

Dr Neath was in his thirties, with curly fair hair, pale-blue eyes and an unassuming manner. As they stood on the doorstep, he shook her hand warmly, smiling as he introduced himself. He had an honest face, she thought, and she felt intuitively that she would be able to rely on him, although she would miss Doctor Wills, who had been their family doctor for as long as she could remember.

'I'm Howard Neath, Dr Wills' replacement,' he told her. 'I believe he explained the situation with regard to his practice.'

'He did, yes. Some time ago, actually, but it has finally come to pass. Do come in.'

The doctor stepped inside and took off his hat, and Lydia hung it on the coat rack. 'His wife's poor health means that he is retiring a little early.'

'Yes, we're all very sorry to lose him, but he has to put his family first. We understand that.' She led Dr Neath into the front room, indicating a chair for him, then sat down and folded her hands in her lap. As always when meeting strangers, Lydia wondered how much this man knew about her unfortunate history but, as always, she did not volunteer anything. Research had reassured her that her marriage to John was legal so she was officially a widow. The extent of the deceit he had carried out had somehow stiffened her to counteract the shock of his death and soften the realization that he had probably never really loved her the way she had imagined.

Lydia and Dr Neath regarded each other from opposite sides of the fireplace as he settled himself in the armchair and put down his black bag. He appeared very at ease, she thought enviously, and found herself imagining him at the funeral of his wife and new-born child.

She said, 'I'm sorry about your family. Losing them both that way must have been terrible for you.'

'It was, of course, but sadly, as a doctor, I have never underestimated the risks posed by childbirth. Too much can go wrong, although we do the best we can and improvements in medical care are better than they have ever been. In spite of that, there is always the unexpected.' He sighed. 'But you, too, have suffered a loss, Mrs Daye, and poor little Adam lost a father who no doubt was dear to him.'

'I think he has survived as well as could be expected. His school teacher says he seems happy, and he doesn't have nightmares or anything.' She looked at him fearfully. 'I would hate to think his life has been blighted in some way that could never be put right. His father would have hated that. I know he loved the boy.'

'I'm sure he did, Mrs Daye. Be reassured on that score. The details are in your family notes, naturally, and I can understand what a setback that must have been for you. Your husband ... his betrayal ... all very fraught. Dr Wills said that you were very brave in the face of such adversity and that he saw little sign of any mental damage to your son.' He smiled. 'He describes you as an excellent mother.'

'He's very kind.' She smiled wryly. 'It was more a case of survival!'

For a moment neither spoke.

'But life goes on,' he said softly. 'We carry on because there is no alternative.'

Lydia nodded – then, fearful that his sympathy would undermine her, she took a deep breath and sat up a little straighter. 'At least we are reasonably secure. That was a worry when my husband died, but our family solicitor helped me untangle the family finances, which sadly were beyond my father. We discovered an endowment plan of which I knew nothing, and it has helped considerably.'

'Money can be bewildering in its complexity!' he agreed.

Just then a large tabby cat slid in at the door and headed straight for the visitor and jumped on to his lap.

'Sooty! Get down.' Lydia jumped to her feet apologetically. 'Let me take him! Many people don't care for cats.'

He made a dismissive gesture, smiling. 'He's fine. Or is it a she? I like cats.'

'My son's beloved tabby is a "he" by the name of Sooty!' She was reminded of her husband's reaction to animal fur, but pushed the unwelcome thought from her. She had long since decided to keep thoughts of John at bay and was relieved that lately, since starting school, the number of Adam's questions about his father had lessened. She had told her son a part truth – that John had been mending a roof, but had fallen and died. Adam still liked to find John's photographs in the album, and Lydia did nothing to discourage him, but she felt it unfair and unnecessary to give him too much unpalatable information. The time for the truth might come later – it might not.

'It is my father who gives me the most concern,' she told the doctor, 'and that is why I have asked you to call. His vagueness is increasing, and he seems depressed. I don't know how I will manage without my friend Dolly, who currently lives with us but will soon be marrying and moving away.'

Lydia refrained from explaining that Dolly, against Lydia's advice, was corresponding with her new fiancé Willis Burke who, given a lighter sentence, was due for release from prison in two weeks' time.

Dr Neath nodded. 'I have been thinking about this problem since Dr Wills discussed it with me, and I have a suggestion to make which—'

Anxiously, she interrupted him. 'Please don't suggest that Father be committed or anything like that! I would never consider it. He is most certainly not mad. He is simply elderly and suffering as many elderly people do with a faulty memory and increasing confusion. He must stay here with us. We are all he has, and I like to think that being among his loved ones—'

It was the doctor's turn to interrupt. 'Such a thing never entered my head, Mrs – er that is...'

'I still call myself Mrs Daye.'

'Mrs Daye. What I want to suggest is that maybe you could employ a nanny who would help keep an eye on your son so that you are able to keep a closer watch on your father.'

Surprised, Lydia considered his idea. 'A nanny? I was thinking more of a part-time nurse.'

'But does your father need *nursing*? Does he feed himself? Wash and dress himself?'

'Oh yes. He is very capable physically, but his mind is unreliable.'

He leaned forward eagerly, and Lydia was struck again by the blue of his eyes. 'I know of a sweet woman – a Miss Spinks – who has been a nanny all her life. She has never been married and is dependent on the family for whom she has been working for the last twenty years. They are now moving to live with the son in France.'

'France? Good heavens.' The idea of some-one choosing to live anywhere else appalled

Lydia.

He smiled. 'The son is a professor of English at a university in Paris and has now obtained a permanent position. His parents are happy to move to be near him and his young family, but Miss Spinks refuses point blank to leave England – she is nearly sixty-five and to her France is almost as remote as another planet!'

'Poor soul!'

'Exactly – so she has nowhere to go.' He regarded her earnestly. 'I would recommend her to you. She would be very loyal, a help with your father and would adore your son. She would also always be there to keep an eye on Adam if you were rushing around the streets in search of your father.' Suddenly aware that perhaps he was leaning too close, he drew back.

'I will certainly give that idea serious thought,' Lydia told him, 'and will come back to you in a day or two.'

He said quickly, 'Tomorrow would be very convenient.'

'Tomorrow it is then.' She smiled, aware of a lift to her spirits. 'Perhaps you would like to come upstairs now and meet my father – he's resting on the bed, but I'm sure he'll come downstairs and join us. I'll make a tray of tea. If you can spare the time, that is. You obviously have other patients...'

'Fifteen minutes would be neither here nor there, Mrs Daye. I would love a cup of tea.'

Fifteen minutes, thought Lydia, wishing it could have been longer. As she made the tea she told herself sternly to calm down, but she still felt ridiculously excited. There had been no other man in her life since her husband's death, and she had scarcely given a thought to her future. The weeks had become months, and the months had lengthened to years, and in all that time she had wrapped herself in a protective coat – Mrs Daye, widow – and now ... Well, was it too late to start again, she wondered, suddenly anxious. Was it even sensible to think that way? John Daye's betrayal had convinced Lydia that she could never trust another man as long as she lived.

'But I dare say there are exceptions,' she murmured, filling the milk jug.

She found some biscuits, arranged them on a plate and added them to the tea tray. As footsteps sounded on the stairs she heard the doctor say something and was surprised to hear her father's laugh ring out. Lydia raised her eyebrows. That was a rare sound. 'But a very welcome one,' she murmured.

As the three of them settled in the front room, Lydia caught the doctor's eye and it seemed to her that a brief look of under-standing passed between them. They had both loved and lost, but did the glance amount to anything, she wondered. Was she imagining it?

By the time that Dolly returned with the children nearly half an hour later, Lydia had convinced herself that when John had betrayed them all those years ago, she had been a little too hasty in thinking her life was over and that she would never love again.

Maybe the worst was over, she thought hopefully and smiled. Perhaps it was time for a new start.